Running *from* Destiny

C.L. Holden

PAGE PUBLISHING, INC.
New York, NY

First originally published by Page Publishing, Inc. 2017

ISBN 978-1-64027-242-2 (Paperback)
ISBN 978-1-64027-243-9 (Digital)

Printed in the United States of America

CHAPTER 1

THE BIG DECISION

The copilot came back to ask everyone to buckle up because they were heading for an unexpected snowstorm over New York. Ronnie became a little nervous. She had never been on a private jet and had never experienced turbulence such as this before. Everyone was very quiet riding through the storm. The captain announced that they would have to make an emergency landing due to ice on the wings. Everyone agreed it was time to pray. All Daphne could think about was sitting in her old room in Bradley, OH, wishing her dad had never taken that job in Mystic, MA. That's all she could think about. She knew she should be praying with the others, but all she could think about was the day her daddy told her the dreadful news that they were leaving.

Daphne wanted to graduate with her class. It was going to be her senior year at Bradley High School, but her dad got a transfer to Mystic, Massachusetts, which meant the Anderson family was moving; moving far away from friends, family, everybody.

Daphne sat in her window looking out at the tall beautiful trees and landscape. "How could Daddy take this job without asking me first?" she thought. "He knows how important senior year is to me. Now I have to make all new friends."

Derek Anderson, forty-five, was the youngest executive at ADT, the Advanced Data Tech Software Company. Derek worked for ADT off and on for the past eighteen years. Being the professional student that he was he had only been full time with the company for seven years but had proven himself well. He was always coming up with fresh, creative ideas.

His boss loved him because he made him rich. Derek had a logical mind that could implement a plan from beginning to end. His projections were always right. He had intuition. He was innovative and the most motivated junior partner in the company. Derek was also ADT's most trustworthy employee. They were making him a full partner with his own franchise.

"What a blessing. Derek Anderson: senior business analyst with my own software store. I can definitely see myself five years from now as CEO in Ohio! We won't be gone that long. Two, three years top. I guess that engineering degree is finally paying off," thought Derek. "Now I can pay off my student loan." They were up to their ears in student loans. That's the only way they could make ends meet with Derek working part time.

Derek and his wife, Ronnie, had been married for twenty-two years. They fell in love in college. Ronnie had gotten her degree in elementary education twenty years ago but never really put it to use outside the home except when she got the chance to work as a third grade teacher for five years while Derek was finishing his degree. Derek now had his master in engineering and bachelor in information systems.

Ronnie was finally a housewife again where she enjoyed making a loving home for her family. She spent her mornings volunteering at each of the kid's schools and always had dinner on the table on time. They decided she would teach for five years so Derek could work part time and concentrate on finishing both his degrees full time. That was five years she thought would never end. Ronnie loved teaching, but she knew her place was in the home, taking care of her family's needs like they agreed before they married. She would say, "I know where my place is. Now if I could just get back to it."

Devon, thirteen, the second oldest, was the tomboy of the family. She could skateboard, Rollerblade, rock climb, and had a mean jump shot. She could beat most of the boys in the neighborhood at any sport. The principal almost cried when he learned he was losing his track star.

DJ (Derek Jr.) was only ten years old. His dad was his hero. They did everything together. His dad had taught him to pitch last summer. He was the starting pitcher of their softball team. He had perfected the curve ball for a kid ten years old; however, Devon could always hit a home run off him. She was the only person he couldn't strike out. That was his goal for the summer to strike her out.

It was Sunday morning, their last service at the Community Christian Church. Pastor Jones regretted losing the Andersons. They were one of his most faithful couples who had raised their children to be a bold witness for Christ. Derek taught them to never be ashamed of God. Pastor Jones preached another one of his powerful sermons that Derek loved so much. They were so convicting. Derek sat there in his seat contemplating on how God had used his life to reach souls. He felt a sudden emptiness.

"How could I leave all of this? Gosh, am I doing the right thing?" he asked himself.

Derek felt that he might have missed his calling. He felt as though he was called to preach ten years ago before he started pursuing his career. Pastor Jones was really disappointed to hear which path Derek chose. Ronnie could tell something was troubling Derek. She reached over for his hand and held it so tenderly. Derek gave her an unconvincing smile.

When service was almost over, Pastor Jones announced that they would be serving cake and punch in the activity room to bid farewell to the Andersons. He could barely look over at Derek. He knew how career minded Derek was, and it would someday come to this moment. Derek was an honest and reliable man who could be trusted. No wonder his company wanted him to go out to the East Coast and straighten things out. He had almost become a professional student in the process. He had been going to school part time for three years on his second bachelor's degree, this time in information systems; then one day he finally decided, "I am tired of working these entry-level positions and getting nowhere. I need to go back to school full time and finish once and for all. Look at all these guys in their twenties coming in here with master's degrees and PhDs passing me up for every promotion."

For the past five years, Derek attended the College for Working Adults, and before he knew it, he had his second bachelors and his master in engineering. He had been offered one of those Silicon Valley jobs, but this new position put him where he wanted to be right now. Derek wanted too many things right now.

CHAPTER 2

MOVING ON UP

It was finally Monday morning, and the Andersons were loading their car. Friends and neighbors were standing around crying, while at the same time happy for them.

"Don't forget to put God first, Derek," said Marcus Grant, Derek's closest friend. "You can't make it without him." Derek and Marcus shook hands and embraced. Derek looked at Marcus and said, "I love you, man. You are my best friend in the world. Promise me you will come up to the Cape and visit us."

"I promise," answered Marcus.

The Andersons drove off, waving and yelling "good-bye" out the window. Derek had to be strong for the whole family. "Alright, everybody, let's dry up those tears and let me see some happy faces. Mystic won't know what to do once the Andersons get to town! It will be no different than Bradley. We will still evangelize and tell everyone about Jesus. We will be the same people, only in a different place."

It took the Andersons two days to get to Mystic since they took their time and enjoyed the scenery and made a vacation out of the trip to their new home.

Derek was right. Mystic didn't know what to do once the Andersons arrived. The town looked eerie. The locals just stood and stared as they drove through town. "Oh great," said Daphne, "Amityville."

There were New Age stores and fortune-telling shops on almost every corner.

"We're not in Kansas anymore," said Ronnie.

"Now, this is no different than any town we've done an outreach at," said Derek. "Remember how strange the people were?"

"Yeah, but those were just visits. We have to *live* here," said Daphne.

"Daphne Lynn Anderson, don't tell me you're afraid of a challenge. You are the boldest teenager I have ever seen. Don't tell me you're going to let the devil put a little fear in you," said Ronnie. "I remember when you used to hold Bible studies during lunch and after school. You started that revival in your junior high and almost caused a heart attack in that teacher, Mr. Wilmington. He did everything he could to get you expelled for sharing the Gospel at school."

"Yeah, the school board didn't know what to do when you started quoting scriptures to them on your rights as a Christian. I love the way you told them that students can recruit occult clubs in the school, but if I mention the name of Jesus, everybody freaks out," Derek added.

Mystic was a small town that was rapidly growing. There was old money and old time locals that had family who had lived in Mystic for centuries. Mystic had a legend of witchcraft and magic, which didn't scare Derek at all. He wasn't afraid of Satan, and he loved a good challenge. Derek planned on turning this town upside down for Jesus. His plan was to get the whole city saved like Jonah.

"Well, here we are, 2537 Glen Oak Drive," said Derek as he parked in front of their new home.

The house was huge. It had five bedrooms with a view right off the lake. It was an old house with a closed in wrap-around front porch. There was an old weeping willow in the front yard.

"It's gorgeous, honey," said Ronnie.

"We can sit on this old front porch and rock our grandbabies, Ronnie," Derek said with a smile.

"I'm too young to even *think* about being a grandmother. I've got at least another twenty years to go," answered Ronnie.

"Yeah, right," said Derek.

DJ loved their huge backyard. There was a shabby tree house in an old oak tree back there. "Just the place to hold camp outs and tell scary stories," thought DJ.

They carried their bags inside. The foyer was breathtaking. The hardwood floors had a quiet creek as they walked. "I guess there won't be any sneaking in past curfew with these floors," Derek said jokingly.

"Curfew? I don't even know what a curfew is! Daddy, you know I have never been on a date in my entire life. All the guys my age at church and at school in Bradley were so scared you would give them the first, second, and third degree they were afraid to even speak to me," replied Daphne.

"Anyway, when you made a copy of that permission to date my daughter application you got from Uncle Marcus and taped it to the back windshield of the van, I think *everyone* got the message."

"I'm not even *interested* in boys, and they won't talk to me, Dad," said Devon. "Some of the boys are afraid to come over and let me kick their butts at sports," she added.

"And that's the way it will be here in Mystic," Derek answered.

Daphne hated to admit it, but she loved her room. She had a window seat that had a view of the lake. Under the window seat was a built-in hope chest. Her room had an antique canopy bed with a matching tall chest, armoire, and vanity. The chest had an old-fashioned lift-top jewelry box built-in. She loved this room. It even had its own bathroom!

"Finally, I don't have to clean up after anyone but myself. No more stepping in DJ's puddles all over the floor when he gets out of the tub. No more waiting for Devon to stop *swimming* in the tub. I can clean it when I want to. Nobody has to see this bathroom but me."

It had a huge old-fashioned tub with claw feet that sat in the middle of the floor. An antique lace shower curtain encircled it. The old-fashioned sink wore a matching lace skirt. There was even an old-fashioned toilet with a pull chain. Daphne felt so special in that room. She had her own room in Bradley, but it was not this elegant, Victorian, and ladylike. To Daphne, it was the room of a princess. "I can't wait until Mom takes me shopping to get a quilt and some more stuff to dress it up. I'm going to send pictures to all my friends in Bradley. They will be so jealous." Just for a moment, Daphne wasn't homesick anymore. She thought maybe she could grow to like this old town.

Ronnie loved the garden out back. It needed a little work, but she had only a little time to get the garden looking good before fall. Ronnie had a green thumb. She could grow anything. She was a true-blue homemaker. There was nothing on earth she probably couldn't fix, cook, or sew. Her girlfriends always told her she should publish a DIY book on all the stuff she knew how to do around the house. "Women would love to have a handy helper around the house written in their own language," they would say. Ronnie thought it would be a great idea to put some things together and send helpful hints to her friends since she wasn't there to advise them or fix stuff for them.

"I'll surprise them and send a quarterly newsletter/blog with my own little helpful hints, recipes and reminders of the seasons," Ronnie thought. "That way, they can tell me what they want to see in the future, and we can stay in touch that way. Imagine. I could get to know the ladies of this town in the same way. I will print my newsletter and distribute it all over town. It will be like a little "mini" almanac. I'll fill it with dinner ideas, cleaning tips, and helpful hints on how to repair things around the house. I'm sure the wives around here have busy husbands too," Ronnie thought out loud. Ronnie felt so fulfilled just then.

The children had six weeks before school would start. It didn't start in Mystic until the day after Labor Day.

"Let's go get some lunch, and we'll drop Dad off at his new office," Ronnie yelled to the children. "We've got plenty of shopping to do, kids. Let's get started with the household stuff today. The rest of our things should be here on Thursday, then we can get settled in and start putting the rest of this stuff away."

CHAPTER 3

THE TOWN

The Andersons decided to have lunch in the town square. It was so mysterious. There was the library that looked at least one thousand years old with vines growing down the sides of its walls. Out front were Gothic statues of gargoyles. DJ did not like the way their eyes followed him as they drove by.

"Where should we eat?" asked Derek.

"I want pizza," yelled Devon.

"No. Let's have fish sticks," answered DJ.

"I don't care as long as we eat before I starve to death," said Daphne sarcastically.

"Can we have a day with no disagreeing?' asked Ronnie. "Honey, just park here, and we will find some place to eat in The Square with a wide variety on the menu so *everyone* can find what they want to eat."

"Listen to you: *The Square*. You've been here a couple of hours, and you're already beginning to sound like a native." Derek said jokingly.

As the Andersons walked through the town square, they noticed there were no fast food restaurants. There was a diner on the corner with a sign in the window: **HAVE YOUR FORTUNE TOLD WHILE YOU EAT**.

"Let's keep going," said Derek. They spotted a lovely restaurant located in the front of a quaint boarding house. The menu was perched in the window.

"Looks like they serve everything. Let's eat here," decided Ronnie.

It was called the Lighthouse Lodge and Cafe. There was an old-fashioned soda fountain and a counter with stools. There were jars on the counter that contained chocolate chip, peanut butter, and sugar cookies. There was also a hot dog machine and a metal rack with assorted flavors of potato chips by the register for eating on the go.

Along the sides of the walls were booths decorated with pine benches and lighthouse decorum all over. The plastic tablecloths had a lace design. Every booth had a lighthouse-shaped candleholder. It was simply charming. The tables seated two, four, or parties of eight. There was a small room to the right that had six banquet-sized tables that sat twelve each. Derek had "business luncheon" on his mind the moment he looked in the room. There was a smaller room with antiques to the left rear of the restaurant with items that were for sale.

CHAPTER 4

THE MEETING

The owner came out to greet the Andersons. "You must be the new family in town. I heard you arrived a couple hours ago. My name is Mildred Lightfoot. I'm a widow. I own this place now. It belonged to my late husband's great-great-grandparents. I sort of inherited it when he died. We started converting it into a bed and breakfast three years ago just before my Howard started getting sick.

"As you can see, I'm not really into antiques like the rest of this town. I'm sure you also noticed the overabundance of New Age all over the place. If you ask me, there is nothing "new" about it. It's plain "old" witchcraft as far as I'm concerned.

"Hello. I'm Derek Anderson. This is my beautiful wife, Ronnie, and our three kids, Daphne, Devon, and DJ."

"DJ, huh? Bet that's short for Derek Jr.," she replied. She was a very wise woman. She had salt and pepper hair that reached past her shoulders and a cute little wrinkled face. She had the friendliest eyes, but it was like she could see right through you as she glared through her wire-framed glasses. She wore a simple plaid dress and sweater although it was late July. She had the kindest handshake. She made the Andersons feel right at home. They felt good about Mildred.

There were six rooms just above the restaurant. It was truly cozy. They were decorated almost exactly like the Anderson's home.

"Look familiar to you?" she asked. "I used to live in the house you just moved in. I decorated it myself. I started that garden in the back of the house too."

"I love it. It looks just beautiful. How is it still so kept up?" asked Ronnie.

"I was still going over once a week and pruning and tilling the soil and watering the trees and stuff like that. I felt that the garden would sell the house by itself if a woman with a green thumb were moving in," she answered. "I sold the house to the bank six months ago, but I missed the garden. Had to keep going over there and keep her up. Oh, I moved out shortly after Howard passed away. Thought I ought to be closer to the B&B, being that I have to get up before sunrise to fix a hearty breakfast and all for my guests."

"Well, you must be hungry with that long drive and all. Let's see what I can whip up special for my new friends the Andersons," she said. Mildred never bothered to give them any menus but kept right on walking into the kitchen area.

"I just love her," said Ronnie. "I feel like I've known her all my life. I bet she's a sweet old grandmother. She is so kind."

Ronnie and her grandmother were very close. She was at her side when she died. Ronnie was only fifteen when her grandmother died, but she can still remember her loving hands and warm smile that could mend any broken heart or scratch or scrape for that matter. Ronnie did not have a close relationship with her mother, though, until a year ago, just before she died.

Mildred returned from the kitchen with a cart full of salads and her own special blend of strawberry lemonade. "I've got Thousand Island, French, Ranch, Italian, and my own special house dressing. What's your pleasure?"

"Of course the House Special," replied Derek. Everyone agreed.

The salads were superb. The crispest greens in a salad you ever saw with beefsteak tomatoes, cucumbers, shredded carrots, green onion, and cheese. The dressing had a hint of strawberry with an Italian taste to it. "I grow my own hot house strawberries; as a matter of fact, everything in this salad is fresh and homegrown. These tomatoes came out of your backyard, Ronnie."

"It's delicious, Mrs. Lightfoot," said Daphne.

"Why thank you, and please, child, just call me Miss Millie," she answered. "We don't need to be formal. We are going to be good friends. I've got a good feeling about you folks."

"Miss Millie, this salad is delicious. I can't wait to see what the main course is," said Derek, turning to Millie who had already exited. "Now where did she go? I didn't even see her leave."

Millie returned shortly with chicken salad on croissants with a mini serving of potato salad and for dessert, pound cake with strawberries. "Miss Millie, you are going to make me gain one hundred pounds because I will be here for lunch quite often if you will be serving food like this every day," said Derek.

"Can I ask you a personal question?" asked Derek. "Where do people serve God around here? I haven't seen but a couple of churches around here, and to be honest, I don't want to go near them."

"Well, I go to a wonderful church in the next town. It's called the Heaven's Door Christian Church. I just started going a little over three years ago, just before my Howard got too sick. Pastor Franks told us we needed to get right with God. We thought we *were* right with God having never murdered anyone or stole anything. We were living good clean lives, no drinking or habits or nothing. But he told us that wasn't good enough to get into heaven. Pastor Franks explained it all to us. Howard and I gave our lives to Jesus right here in the restaurant in front of our customers, and we were in regular attendance until Howard got down really bad. When Howard got sick, he visited him almost every day at the house; and when he went into the hospital, he was right there with me when he died. Pastor Franks did such a lovely memorial service for my husband.

A lot of the congregation would come by and pray for him, but we all knew it was time for Howard to go on and meet the Lord. I am so thankful that God sent Pastor Franks into my restaurant when he drove through our little town of Mystic. They still come over and evangelize the first Saturday of every month. The church is only twenty minutes from here off the main highway. I spend practically all day there on Sunday, and there is also service on Wednesday nights. Why don't you come with me on Sunday? I'll introduce you to the congregation. If you're in the square on Saturdays, you might see some of them passing out flyers to the heathens of this town. People can be so bitter and religious. Sometimes, they get thrown out of the square by different storeowners, but we need them here spreading the 'good word.' There is nothing else godly going on around here with all of this new and improved religion. It just makes me sick."

"Are there young people in the congregation, Miss Millie?" asked Daphne.

"Tons of them ranging from birth to about twenty-five. The teens are all fired up. They are not ashamed to tell people about Jesus," answered Millie.

"From what I understand one of the young men at the high school got suspended for three days last year for preaching in the cafeteria. They said he was disrupting the school and forcing Jesus down their throats. They took the school to court and won. Now they're trying to get permission to hold an after school Bible club just like they have the foreign language clubs and craft clubs after school."

"Sounds like a challenge to me," said Daphne. "How many kids in this town go to the church?"

"Not very many. Their parents didn't convert, so they don't allow the kids to go. We've got some practitioners of the occult here in this town, and they are not willing to give that up. If you have a pet, don't let him out alone at night. I've heard some strange stories about what goes on around here during Halloween too," answered Millie.

"Well, we come from a Satan hating, God fearing, Holy Ghost preaching church in Bradley, Ohio," replied Derek.

"Bradley, Ohio?" asked Millie. "I was raised in Brookfield, Ohio, along with my sister, Gertie Sims. Gertie and I lost touch with each other over the past forty years. She was my big sister. She did not speak to me after I married and moved away because Howard asked me to marry him. Gertie used to follow Howard around, and he didn't like that. He liked quiet girls. I never gave him a second thought. I was such a bookworm. One day, he came over, and I thought he was there to see Gertie, and he asked my dad for permission to take me out for an ice cream with my parents along of course. I refused because I knew how Gertie felt about him. For the next six months, Gertie kept dating a bunch of different guys trying to make Howard jealous. This only made him want her less. I finally said yes and went out with him for ice cream with my parents. I fell in love with him, and he got sent away to war. I thought I would never see him again, but I waited for him. Two years later, Howard showed up at my door with an engagement ring and asked my father if he would allow me to marry him. He was on a month long furlough, and we got married in two weeks, and we had a two-week honeymoon since he had to ship off again. Howard got injured a year later and was sent home after having his hip replaced. We were never able to have children, so we traveled. I've been to so many countries. Gertie hadn't spoken to me since the day we went for ice cream. She supposedly married and moved to some town in Minnesota about thirty-five years ago and had three daughters. Howard and I never had any children, so she always said that God cursed us because I stole her husband. I used to believe that she had cursed us too. She always spoke evil about us.

Finally one day out of the blue, I got a letter she had written on her deathbed. She told me she had given her life to Jesus, and she wanted me to forgive her for not speaking to me all these years, and that she loved me and urged me to get my life right too. I couldn't write her back because she was already gone when I got the letter. I miss her so much. We used to be so close when we were in high school and all the way up to the day Howard came by. I wanted her to know that I had given my life to Jesus too. If I could've just met my nieces," she said sadly.

Ronnie burst into tears stating, "I'm Veronica, the oldest of Gertie's daughters. My maiden name is Sims. You must be my Aunt Mildred Mom used to speak of all the time. She was so prideful for many years. She never wanted to speak to you. You're right. She hated you for the longest time. She was jealous because you were chosen for his wife instead of her. I never knew my uncle's name because she always talked about 'that man' and your Aunt Mildred."

Ronnie continued, "She resented the fact that she knew him first, but he chose you. She would always tell Victoria and Valerie and me to never betray one another like Aunt Mildred did her and never let a man come between us. I always wanted to meet you, but she would never tell us where you lived. We never knew your husband's name or your last name. She never would keep any old paperwork or photos around the house because she did not want us to try to contact you. Believe me, you would have been at her memorial service. Pastor Jones did a wonderful eulogy on how she traded in her hatred and bitterness and forgave her sister in the end. He told her she had to let you know she forgave you, and that's the letter she finished just before she died. I guess her attorney must've found you because you got the letter she wrote. She gave her life to Jesus just like Uncle Howard a year before she died. Derek and I would witness to her on a daily basis trying to break through that wall of hatred she had built for over forty years. Then one day, she just showed up in church, went to the altar and bowed her knee to Jesus and died a true Christian. I was so thankful to God for answering our prayers because not long after she turned her life around, we found out that she had a terminal case of sclerosis of the liver from drinking. She died happy though. You wouldn't have known she was so bad off until about two weeks before her death. She always had a smile and a good disposition about her and told people (don't worry about me, I'm goin' home!) And Glory to God, now I get to meet my Aunt Mildred. How on Earth can people deny the power of God?"

Millie asked, "Where are Victoria and Valerie?" Wiping the tears of joy from her eyes.

"Victoria is in college. She is studying medicine. She says she wants to find a cure for what Mom died of. She is so absorbed in her studies. She only believes in science. She is a man hater and has no interest in them whatsoever. She hangs around a bunch of men hating women.

"Mom never raised us in church. I came to know Jesus through Derek. I met him in college, and he had been attending the church we just left in Ohio, and he witnessed to a group of us, and I immediately wanted what he had: peace of mind. We got married a year later.

"Valerie is married to a man who is never at home. They have two children, Allegiance, their ten-year-old daughter and a son, Liberty, who is eight. Her husband, Alan, is an ambulance-chasing crook. He is a very dishonest and money-hungry lawyer. She doesn't care because he leaves her the ATM card, checkbook, and several credit cards with a hefty allowance, so she pretends that money can buy her happiness. Her children attend private boarding schools, so she never sees them except for *selective* weekends and holidays. She spends all the time at their country club with the other attorney's wives who feed her head with all kinds of nonsense and garbage and tell her how to run her marriage."

"Aunt Mildred, we have so much to catch up on. I've got pictures of me and my sisters as we were growing up and pictures of Mom and Dad. My dad left us when we were all in junior high school. I don't know where he is now. Mom was so bitter he couldn't stand to live with her. He would send money from time to time and each time he was living in a different state. My mom moved back to Ohio from Minnesota when I was in the tenth grade, just before Grandma passed away. I last saw him at my wedding twenty-two years ago. He showed up drunk. I was so embarrassed. One of the men from our church had to give me away. My father was in his car drunk and asleep; then he woke up during the reception and was mad because we weren't serving liquor."

"What a wonderful testimony, Veronica," said Millie. "You must let people know you can still serve God after all that hatred and rejection from your childhood. I was at Mom's funeral, but Gertie would not introduce me to my nieces. She sent word that if I tried to come near any of you, I would regret it. I got a friend to take pictures of you three, but Gertie found out and smashed my camera to bits. She had spies all over that funeral."

"Aunt Mildred, Derek can tell you, I was just like Mom and Victoria. I didn't trust men. I had an attitude all the time. I used to see him around campus and wonder: *what is this fool so happy about? Nobody is this happy.* Then one day, he was witnessing to a group of us, and I truly listened to what he had to say and just like that, Jesus changed my bitterness to sweetness. I suddenly had love for people. I started going out and telling other people about what Jesus had done for me and here we are. We have raised our children to be the same way," stated Ronnie.

They all embraced, and everyone in the restaurant was practically in tears. There was a man at the counter, Jackson Sanders, from the local newspaper, *The Mystic Gazette*, and he asked if he could do a piece on them for Sunday's Family section of the paper. They all agreed.

CHAPTER 5

WHO'S IN CHARGE?

Derek was astonished with his plush new office. When the Andersons arrived, there was a huge banner above his desk that read: *Welcome to Mystic!* He had an administrative assistant, four clerical workers, and four sales associates. Everyone introduced themselves to the Andersons.

Derek had a large mahogany desk with the most comfortable leather chair behind it. DJ sat in his dad's chair. "I could live in this chair, Dad," he said. On Derek's credenza in his office was a huge basket filled with fruits, salty snacks, cheeses, crackers, and a bottle of champagne. There was a fully stocked bar in his office. Sitting to the right of the entrance of Derek's office was a large burgundy, leather sofa that matched his chair.

Next to Derek's office was an executive conference room, which was decorated in leather also. There was a plasma TV and projector screens on the walls. Down the hall was the break room the size of a small café with a stove, refrigerator, microwave, and four small tables. There was another huge TV in the corner with a love seat in front of it.

"Honey, why don't you and the kids go shopping for a couple of hours and let me get settled in and get to know my staff a little bit. Call me on the cell phone when you are on your way here, and I'll take you and the kids out for a celebration dinner," said Derek. He kissed Ronnie and the children good-bye.

Derek called a meeting with his staff to go over his expectations and goals for the company. Charity, the administrative assistant, was going to be Derek's right hand. She had been with the East Coast office for over ten years. Derek had only corresponded with Charity through e-mail and played phone tag with her for the past two months. She was the one who had decorated Derek's office. Charity was twice divorced with no kids, and she was man crazy. She dressed trashy. Too much cleavage, but not enough length on her skirts, along with gaudy jewelry, too much makeup, and tons of hair spray in her bird's-nest-looking hairstyle.

Charity did not have time for a husband or family, and she had once thought of becoming a salesperson, but she liked working for powerful men much better. Sitting in on private board meetings in a room full of rich men who never spent any time with their wives was the drug of her choice.

The former sales manager, Roger Sampson, was forced to retire early. He had misappropriated funds and had almost driven that division into bankruptcy. He had made a hefty amount of personal money with ADT and felt he was God's gift to all women. He never spent time with his family anymore. He was always flirting with Charity, buying her gifts and taking her out to dinner and on "business trips," misusing the corporate accounts on her. He was also semi-involved with a woman on the other side of town whose husband was away all the time on offshore drilling jobs and was only home once a month.

Roger had a mild stroke six months earlier, and Derek was chosen to come in and take over the East Coast operations. It became apparent to Derek he had given Charity too much responsibility in the office, and Derek knew he would have to put her in her place.

"I know that women have a good business sense and are some of the best deal closers; however, this company will be run like my home, with respect for headship, and under the direction and guidance of God," Derek said to himself.

"OK, Mr. Big, Strong, Boss said Charity (in a Mae West type dialect and body motions) let's get this meeting to order."

"Thank you, Charity," said Derek.

"Please, everyone, sit down. Charity is passing out packets I prepared for everyone. Read it in your spare time. It will be your office manual. We will go over this section by section on a weekly basis starting next week."

"First of all, I would like to say thank you to everyone for welcoming my family to your town and to this location. The warm reception was greatly appreciated—"

"Well, if you must know, I did *all* the preparations and decorating of the office for your arrival," boasted Charity, interrupting Derek.

"As I said previously, thank you to *everyone involved* from the biggest to smallest detail. My family truly appreciates you," answered Derek.

Derek continued, "I will need to see each one of you individually in my office after this meeting to go over the details of your job descriptions and expectations. Charity, we will start with you immediately after the meeting. Now, what are the projections for the coming fiscal year?" Derek asked Michael Roper, the lead sales associate. Mike began to read off his projections to the group. Derek listened and looked around the table to see who was paying attention. Charity was playing with the ruffles in her collar of her low-cut blouse, and her many bracelets were banging and clanging like soft wind chimes. Derek gave her "the look." Charity smiled at him. She loved the attention.

As Derek started speaking to the group, Charity was thinking to herself, "I don't think this one will be so easy. He doesn't look at me the way that Roger used to. He didn't even acknowledge how I'm dressed, and he won't even look at my body. He must be bisexual. Come on. Look at me. I am gorgeous. What's wrong with this guy? Is he blind or what?" Charity seductively stared at Derek while he was still speaking to the group looking him right in the face trying to make eye contact with him. Derek glanced over at her as if she was another piece of furniture in the room.

"Yep. Something's got to be wrong with him if he doesn't want *this*," Charity said under her breath.

"First of all, I want to tell everyone that I am a Christian. This means that I expect, no, I *demand* respect in this office. Let's be mindful of our profanity. There are ladies present here. It is not a necessary tool anywhere I can think of. I do not drink. I'm a recovering alcoholic. Thank you for the bottle of wine; however, I prefer sparkling cider or ginger ale. We can use that bottle of wine to christen the yacht when we sail off on one if our many cruises down the Atlantic Ocean *with our families* when we land that big deal down the road. Yes, I think big. And I see only the positive for the future. I've seen what all of you can do. I know we will put Mystic on the map as far as ADT is concerned.

"I expect integrity out of each of my employees, and I also believe in rewarding good work. That's how I got where I am today.

"I have nothing but the utmost respect for anyone who will step out, be responsible *and* accountable for his or her actions. We all make mistakes. I expect a mistake to be brought out in the open and not covered up. We all go down if this happens. When the company loses, we all lose in the long run. I did not take this job with the expectation of micromanaging or becoming anyone's babysitter.

"We will have our business luncheons during the last week of each month to keep each other abreast of what the other person is working on. I expect you to come to all meetings with fresh ideas and prepared to let the group in on whatever special projects you are working on. Expect to spend a maximum of ten minutes each on what you are working on, what you have accomplished and what your prospects are for future projects. I know it sounds intimidating to have to speak publicly, but believe me, it will prepare you for the future. I expect everyone to be on time. I will not be sitting next to the door or playing watchdog. I will expect you to honestly manage your time out of the office. These are salaried positions, so there is no time clock to punch. We work on the honor system.

"There is so much money and bonuses to be made here. It is up to each and everyone on my sales team to seek those bonuses. The administrative staff will be involved in a bonus program also. You will be assigned personally to a sales person. Keep a log of all of your contacts and everything you do for your salesperson. At the end of each month, you too will be rewarded based on your salesperson's productivity. So it is up to each of you to work as a team to make the deal go through. Make sure your spreadsheets are up to date with current figures. I expect you to keep in your log the status of your contacts, so that if you become ill, God forbid, or an unexpected emergency arises, *anyone* can come behind you and pick up right where you are.

"Integrity, responsibility, innovation, and giving 200 percent is what I base my merit system on. I do not expect anyone to work overtime or weekends. I do expect you to do as much as you can in a day so that you can go home to your families without stress. I feel that stress slows down productivity and encourages chaos. Look at how it almost brought down this division. We are not here to 'grand stand' one another; however, there may be times when we will recognize employees that go that extra mile. We will come up with an innovations reward program together. The name of the game here is for the East Coast to be the very best for ADT. Are there any questions before I call each one of you into my office?" No one responded. Everyone looked around at each other to see if anyone had raised his or her hand. "Well, as I said, I will start with Charity, my *executive assistant*. Yes. I am promoting Charity to executive assistant and promoting the clerical staff to administrative assistants. Charity, follow me, please," Derek replied. The administrative assistants smiled at each other.

As Charity followed Derek into his office, she was wondering why she could never find a man with qualities like this. "Why are all the good ones always married?" thought Charity. "I hope his wife realizes what a good man she has. I hope she recognizes a woman like me would love to take care of a man like this. He is every single woman's dream come true."

"Have a seat, Mrs. Foster," said Derek, turning to Charity.

"Excuuuse meee," sang Charity, as she raised and slightly waved her hands like a beauty queen. "Mrs. Foster is my mother. Uhm, I prefer to be called Charity. Besides, it's *Ms.* Foster. I gave up the name *Mrs.*, when I got divorced from *Mr.* Peterson," said Charity, as she attempted to close the door to Derek's office.

"And keep the door open, please. Charity, I would like to get a few things straightened out and on the table with you. First of all, I think we will have to be a little more formal around here. I would like for you to address me as Mr. Anderson from this day forward. It's not a power thing. I just feel that the best thing for a work relationship is if the executive assistant addresses her superior as Mr. Besides, it will help you to maintain professionalism in the manner of which you answer the phones around here and greet clients. As a matter of fact, I would like you to address all of our male associates as Mr.

"And while we are on the subject, your duties as executive assistant are as follows: you will assist in answering all phones with preference to my line first. You will screen and announce all calls, implement and maintain the record keeping system for the sales associates and their administrative assistants, handle all weekly payroll duties with the assistance of the most senior administrative assistant. You will type correspondence as needed and assist in *my* sales, that's where your bonuses come from, and you will be cross-training the other administrative assistants to perform your duties when you are not here. It is not good for only one person to do a specific job. You will also sit in on my private business meetings sitting at the rear of the table in the conference room, and you will have the minutes transcribed to me no later than twenty-four hours after the meetings unless specified otherwise. I have increased your salary by 20 percent.

"Secondly, we don't want anyone coming into this office to get the wrong impression. First impression means so much to the integrity of ADT. Starting Monday morning, I would like you to dress in a more professional manner. I will be posting a dress code for the office on the bulletin board in the cafeteria. We don't want anyone to feel uncomfortable, offended, nor violated by the way anyone dresses or conducts themselves. I will be having this conversation with every other member of personnel as well. Are we clear on this issue, Ms. Foster?" Charity looked down and only nodded her head affirmatively. "I think we will make a good team here. I have heard nothing but great things about you and your excellent skills of managing this office. I am looking forward to working with each and every one of you. I believe we can make a difference in the East Coast.

"You can have the rest of the day off. Enjoy your weekend. Send in the most senior of the administrative assistants as you leave."

"Thank you for believing in me, Mr. Anderson. You have a nice weekend also," Charity replied.

As Derek finished meeting individually with all of the staff, he was in the office alone. Derek felt so important. He had finally hit the big time. He made a call to Pastor Jones. They prayed together. He invited Pastor Jones and his family to come to Mystic to stay a day or two. "When I come to do that revival in Cape Cod, I'll come by and visit. Never stop praying and find a spirit-filled, Gospel-preaching church immediately, Derek," said Pastor Jones before he hung up.

The cell phone rang. It was Ronnie and the kids. "Honey, are you ready to go get some dinner? The kids are getting restless and hungry. We spent plenty of money on supplies for the house. I could really enjoy this, Derek. I like not having to worry about how much something costs. Don't worry. I am still looking for bargains. I'm just buying every bargain I see! No more saying I wish I could have bought this or that—I'm buying it all! Just wait until I find the main department stores. We found the mall—it was ten minutes away. We should be there in about thirty minutes. Daphne was finally at the register, and she was almost done. 'Gotta go. Love ya. Bye." Ronnie hung up the phone.

CHAPTER 6

GETTING TO KNOW YOU

The Andersons went to a neighborhood pizza place. It was a little hole in the wall place with lots of character and pictures of Sicily and Venice hanging on the walls. Groups of teenagers were hanging out all over the place. As Daphne and Devon returned from the restroom, a young man who looked to be about seventeen or eighteen approached them.

"Hi. I'm Stuart. Everybody calls me Stu. I go to Mystic High School...," Daphne and Devon said hello and kept on walking. Stuart followed them to the table. He looked over at Derek who was looking sternly at him as if to say, "Take one more step toward my daughters, and I will break both of your legs."

Derek stood up and said, "Hello, my name is Derek Anderson. I believe you just met my two daughters. Is there something I can help you with young man?"

"No, sir," answered Stuart. "I...uh...just wanted to know their names and what schools they will be going to."

"Their names are not important. What is your intention for following them back to this table and disrupting our dinner? Are you serving God, young man? And if you are, what are you doing disrespectfully hounding my daughters?" Derek demanded.

"What?" asked Stuart.

"Church? Nobody around here goes to church. Didn't you know this is Witch Country? My grandmother is a midwife and a psychic healer. My mom owns the Curiosity Shoppe on the corner over there. Where y'all from, Kansas?"

"What you fail to understand, young man, is that my daughters may look like fresh meat to you, but you are barking up the wrong tree. They do not fall for a line from *any* boy. They are not looking for a boyfriend or a date for the prom."

"Can they talk for themselves, old dude?" asked Stuart.

Daphne interrupted, "Daddy, may I?"

"Go ahead, pumpkin," sighed Derek, shaking his head at Stuart.

"Stuart, first of all, I do not appreciate you following me and my sister to our table. If you ever want to be friends with me, you will learn how to dress, talk, and conduct yourself in the presence of a lady. Like my father said, I am not looking for a boyfriend. The man I date will be the man I will marry. Now, apologize to my family for disrupting our dinner."

At first, Stuart just stood there with a blank stare on his face. "Uh, I was just admiring how you guys were sitting at the table getting along without yelling and screaming at each other. I don't even have a family to go out to dinner with, and when we were together, we never sat down to dinner. No one even cooks dinner. My old man ran out on us when I was seven. My mom reads tarot cards every day looking and hoping for Mr. Right. How can you be so happy? Or are you just a table of fakes? If not, I want what you guys got whatever it is."

"Son, we all have problems," Derek replied. "There is no perfect anything except Jesus Christ. We are still together because we made God the foundation of our lives. We put him first. Then comes family. If God is first in your life and you are praying, reading his word, seeking his word by attending church regularly and obeying that which is taught, you can't help but have a healthy, happy home. It does not happen overnight. You have to work at it. Appears to me like you have no hope, but I know where you can get some faith and have hope restored. Right here and now. Do you want to pray with me?" Derek asked.

"Right here in the pizza place? In front of my friends?" Stuart asked.

"Jesus died publicly, so why can't you receive him publicly? He can come into your heart right now with just one heartfelt prayer. Who cares what your friends think? You can leave this place tonight knowing that if *you* died in *your* sleep, you would make heaven your home. So how about it?" Derek asked.

"OK," said Stuart. The Andersons prayed with Stuart. He stayed at the table with them and had dinner with them. Derek and Ronnie both gave their testimonies about how Jesus changed their lives. Daphne testified about how she ignored her friends who made fun of her for being a virgin.

"I just know I have something to give my husband on my wedding night that they can never give," Daphne replied.

"Wow. I'm really a virgin too," whispered Stuart. "My friends think I'm not. I was too embarrassed to tell them that I wasn't. I haven't gone all the way, but I've gotten pretty close. I like to hang out with the guys, and we talk filth about girls. If they knew I was a virgin, I would get a royal butt kicking every day like the rest of nerds we pick on at school."

Derek said, "Well, it's time to come clean. They just watched you give your life to Jesus. Why not put all your cards on the table. You don't need friends like that anyway. Now you need to go and tell somebody what Jesus has done for you. I'll come with you."

"Hey, preacher boy. What you doing over there?" asked one of the boys.

"Cut it out, Cameron," answered Stuart. "I just got the goods. I just asked Jesus to come into my heart and be my Lord and Savior. If I die tonight, I go to heaven. Where y'all gonna go if you die tonight?"

"Straight to hell where my grandfather, my father, and brother are." Cameron laughed. "We're gonna have one big party down there—"

Derek interrupted Cameron. "You've got the wrong idea about hell, young man. You think hell's gonna be fun? Have you read what the Bible says about hell? It is forever. If you were to die tonight, did you know the kind of hell you will spend eternity in has total darkness, tormenting demons, and a lake of fire that is hotter than anything you could ever imagine? I don't think there is no one in hell raising a glass toasting the devil.

"As a matter of fact, the devil is laughing at them while he torments them. Now if that sounds like fun to you, then you need to pray for some new brain cells also."

Cameron asked, "How do you know so much about hell?"

"I read the Bible *every day*," answered Derek. "Staying in the word and talking to God daily is the only way to make it in your Christian walk."

"No thanks," said Cameron. "I'm too young to be acting like some old dried up Holy Roller. Stu, you are so out of the club, man. Don't come around any of us with that Jesus crap, preacher boy."

"I'll be praying for all of you," said Derek.

"Me too," Stuart added. Cameron and his friends walked out of the pizza place. Stuart watched his friends leave with no regrets.

"That felt good," he replied. "I thought I couldn't live without those guys. We have hung together since I was ten years old terrorizing the Town Square tourists and menacing every neighborhood we could. Shop owners hate to see us coming. I have stolen so much stuff in the past seven or eight years. Stuff I didn't even need or want. I just took it so my friends would think I was cool. I can't count the number of girls I have violated and told them I liked them and the God-awful things I have forced them to do to me and with me. How can God forgive me for all of that? I only deserve hell, Mr. and Mrs. Anderson."

Derek put his hand on Stuart's shoulder and told him, "We all deserve hell. The whole Earth is wicked. In our thoughts and our deeds. We are all born in sin. What you've just become is called born again in the Christian world. There is no other way to enter into heaven. And yet, even if you had never done any of the things you just discussed with me and had never given your life to Jesus, you could still die and go to hell. You see, the Bible says no man cometh unto the Father except through Jesus Christ. He is the only way. Stuart, God has forgiven you for all of those things in your past. What you just did was to repent and confessed Christ as your Lord and Savior. You have a clean slate with him now. It is as if it never happened. Isn't God good, son? As long as you continue to serve Jesus and make him first in your life, you will spend eternity in heaven with Jesus and the rest of the saints of God who have gone on before us who gave their lives to him."

"Wow," said Stuart. "You mean everything I have ever done up to this moment is forgiven? What if I had killed someone? By the way, I never have, but what about murderers? They will see heaven if they repent too?"

"Absolutely," answered Derek. "I used to be a little hell raiser myself when I was about your age. I was so full of rage, and I hated my home life, so I wanted to take my anger out on people who had a good life. If you had money and lived in a good neighborhood I would rob you or break into your house. I could have and should have been shot and dead and rotting in hell by now, but I am *so thankful* (he looked up)… that God gave me another chance. He saw the good in me when I felt there was nothing else."

"But, Mr. Anderson, you don't look like a thug like I do," Stuart said.

"You think I always looked like this? I used to walk around wearing gangster and pimp wannabe clothes. I wore gold chains that weren't even mine. I had stolen every one of them. I carried around brass knuckles and switchblades to scare women into giving me their purses. One feisty little old lady almost scratched my eyes out one day though. She said, '*I ought to put you over my knee. I got grand-children your age. Don't think I won't.*' She slapped me up and down my big head. She told me, '*Boy, you need Jesus! You better get yourself straightened up before you end up in jail or in the cemetery.*' Well, that night, I couldn't sleep. I tossed and I turned and I kept hearing, '*Boy, you need Jesus, you need Jesus,*' all night long ringing in my mind. I was nineteen years old. I had dropped out of high school two years earlier and wasn't doing a thing with my life but wasting it. That fall, I got my GED, enrolled in City College, and this guy witnessed to me on campus. I gave my life to Jesus and look at me now. I am a successful businessman but not by any of my own doing. I give all the credit to my Heavenly Father. He put me in my right mind, got me off the streets and on the right track with my life. I would see some of my old friends when I was back home in Ohio. They are doing the same old thing. Stealing, getting high, drinking all day and doing nothing with their lives like I was. Some of them are dead. I had witnessed to them, and they told me to get lost. One of my friends did call me when he found out he had throat cancer from smoking and drinking so much homemade moonshine liquor. He died a year ago. I can't say where he is right now. But I do know that he got a second chance and didn't take full advantage of it. The doctors gave him six months to live, and God gave him two more years instead. What he did with those two years would have been the most important decision he could ever make in his whole life. What I'm trying to say Stuart is today is the day of salvation. Start reading your Bible and get to know Jesus *personally*. It can happen. You can have a personal relationship with him." Stuart just stood in amazement listening to Derek's dynamic testimony. "I have so many stories and experiences to share with you. Do you realize that you, Daphne, and Devon could make such an impact in that school? You have to go in from day one and be a bold witness for Jesus. Let people know where you stand. Let them know you are a changed man. Give them the Gospel of Jesus Christ. Never be ashamed of him, and he will not be ashamed of you on Judgment Day," said Derek.

Stuart asked, "How do people on the job react to you? So many adults are doing their own thing drinking, partying, and having affairs. How do you get the Gospel across to them?"

Derek answered, "A saved adult is the same as a saved teenager and vice versa. Teenage sexual immorality is the same as adult sexual immorality. The sin is the same. There is no such thing as a *little* sin. Sin is sin. It will keep growing and growing. Before you know it, you will go on to bigger things, and you'll be in too deep. But the glory of it all is that you gave your life to Jesus before it was too late; he just wiped the slate clean. Everything from the past is forgiven. That's what I tell adults. I know they are bound in some wicked stuff, like perversion on the Internet, secret chat rooms, getting high and sexual sin of extramarital affairs, but I just tell them just like I told you God can forgive all that, and you can start clean. Most people haven't even heard the Gospel because it is not being preached in their churches. They think because they go to church on Sunday everything is OK. Well, when I tell them that good works and going to church on Sunday is not enough, they want to know more. God wants us to keep our bodies pure and holy. That includes drugs and overindulging in alcohol. There is so much to learn if you get in a Gospel preaching church. You cannot learn it all at home watching TV church. That's not to say that people who are shut in can't go to heaven either. God knows their situations. You need to hear sermons preached over a pulpit and feel the conviction in the room. That's what I loved about my church back home. We did not miss a service. God was going to be there, and he may have something to tell me, and I didn't want to miss one word." Just then, Derek felt his own conviction about leaving his hometown and church.

It was almost eight o'clock and time for the Andersons to leave the pizza place. "Do you want a ride home?" Derek asked Stuart.

"No. I live right around the corner. I'll walk home so I can think on all this new stuff," Stuart answered.

"Come out to the car with me, and I'll give you a Bible you can start reading. I will pick you up for church at 8:00 on Sunday morning, Stuart," said Derek. "Here's our number. Leave a message on the answering machine with your address tomorrow."

When Stuart got home, he read the Bible. It was the first time he had ever held a Bible in his hands. He had been in church for funerals, but he had never really paid attention. He was amazed at how much the Bible made sense to him now. It was becoming so vivid. He couldn't put the book down. He read story after story. He read for two hours starting with Adam and Eve. He flipped back and forth and read about Moses. He read about Abraham and Sarah. He found the story about Noah and the Ark. He was fascinated with the story of David. Stuart could not believe how God used such common people in the Bible. He was a little embarrassed about going to church because he didn't have any decent clothes. Every garment he owned was baggy and saggy. Stuart knew he couldn't let that stand in his way. He wanted to go to church to meet God in his house and feel his presence like Derek described in the restaurant. That night, Stuart dreamed of heaven. It was the most beautiful place. There were streets of gold and angels singing.… The people in heaven were so radiant. Everyone wore white and looked so pure. It was as if they glowed in the dark. He did not see God in his dream, but he knew where he was in the dream, sitting on a throne like the Bible described with angels surrounding him singing praises.

CHAPTER 7

SUNDAY GO TO MEETING

"Kids, get up! Breakfast is ready!" yelled Ronnie.

"Oh, man. Isn't this supposed to be summer vacation?" thought Daphne, as she rolled over throwing the covers over her head.

Two minutes passed, and Derek yelled, "Your mother said breakfast is ready. Everyone front and center!" Daphne leapt out of bed. Devon jumped straight up practically falling out of her bed, and DJ sprang out of bed, grabbing his robe and flying down the stairs.

"Did you wash your face, young man?" Derek asked.

"No, sir. You said front and center. I wanted to get down here as fast as I could," DJ answered.

"Well, get in that bathroom and please wash your face *and* hands quickly. Don't leave a mess for your mother either." Derek demanded. Daphne came floating down the stairs like a beauty queen in her new pink satin PJs and flowing robe.

"I haven't slept this great in a long time. I didn't hear any traffic or loud music all night. I slept like a log. I could hear the crickets, and occasionally, I would hear a dog bark. I could come to love this country life," she added.

"You aren't even close to living in the country," said Ronnie. "There isn't a farm around for miles. Where your father and I grew up that was country life."

"I know, I know, and you walked twenty-five miles uphill to school and carried your lunch, and everyone sat in the same classroom, and Nellie Olsen would pick on everyone," interrupted Daphne.

"That was on *Little House on the Prairie!* I went to urban schools just like you do now. I took my lunch some days, and I bought lunch at school too. It was more nutritious than that junk they feed your kids today. We had soup and grilled cheese sandwiches. There would be meatloaf, mashed potatoes and gravy, spaghetti with meatballs, garlic bread and salad. And that included dessert and your drink for about seventy-five cents a day. It was none of that fast food, soda machines and potato chips you guys like to eat all day and then come home and raid the refrigerator because you're starving. I can't wait until school starts, so I can see what parent volunteer programs they have out here," answered Ronnie.

"No, Mom, you are *not* going to embarrass me at school. Are you?" Daphne pleaded. "If you call letting the staff know that I don't intend there to be any pornographic materials in the libraries, then yes, I plan to embarrass you. Get ready Mystic High School. Here comes Ronnie. If they didn't plant all that junk in kids' minds, they wouldn't be so experimental and don't get me started on the STDs," she replied.

"Mom. Okay. We get the point," Daphne mumbled. "Can we just eat?"

Ronnie had prepared a bountiful breakfast. There were scrambled eggs, pancakes, bacon *and* sausage, grits, fruit, milk and freshly squeezed orange juice. "You really outdid yourself, honey," said Derek.

"What are you trying to make me get all fat and out of shape?"

"No, I want you to never forget that everything you need or think you might need is right here at home, honey. I expect to see my husband for breakfast and dinner on a regular basis. I don't plan on raising three kids all alone. I didn't marry you or follow you to Mystic to become a single parent."

"K?" Ronnie answered.

"I guess she told you too, Dad," replied Daphne.

"I guess she did," answered Derek. "Now get finished eating so we can get ready for church." The Andersons finished their breakfast in silence.

The church was a converted old barn. It had fine dark pine pews and hardwood floors. When the Andersons walked in, they were greeted so warmly and friendly. "This church reminds me of back home. The people know how to make you feel welcome," thought Derek.

"You must be the Andersons. I am Pastor Franks. Welcome to Heaven's Door Christian Church. Miss Millie has told us so much about you. I hope you haven't prepared dinner because the congregation has prepared a potluck to welcome your family. I have already spoke with your pastor from Bradley, Ohio, and I can't wait to meet him at the Cape Cod revival. Have a seat! Get to know us! We already know about you, thanks to Miss Millie. How blessed she is to have family here with her now. I am so delighted to see you folks come right out after just moving here three days ago. I must say you are more committed than some of our regular members. Now, who is this young man with you? I thought you only had one small boy."

"Pastor Franks, this is my newest convert, Stuart Jefferson," answered Derek.

"We met him Friday night at the pizza joint. He gave his life to Jesus right in front of his hoodlum friends, and I must say he is hungry for the word. He asked me a million questions about the Bible all the way here. We're hoping to convert some of the other kids at the high school. I'm planning outreaches, movies, car washes, you name it, to get the word of God out to the people of Mystic."

"Derek, I wish I had a hundred disciples like you. I can't get much participation. Everyone is so career minded and self-involved. I can't get the men out of their woodworking garages or off the Internet long enough to carry out a decent outreach. My young men are doing it all. The age group from seventeen to thirty is having revival. I guess everyone else thinks they have put their time in already. The Kingdom of God does not have a retirement program. I try to instill that in my entire congregation. Where has the church gone wrong?" he asked.

"It's not just the church, Pastor," answered Derek. "Men feel that they should sit on the sidelines after a few years of getting too comfortable. I never allowed my family to get comfortable. I know who I used to be. I know what God saved me from. I never want to go back to the life I once had. I can only imagine how terrible hell is, and I don't want to prove myself right. Just keep on preaching the Gospel, and maybe someday, they will hearken their hearts to the word once again and get back on fire. It won't take gimmicks to win them back either. It will take some convicting preaching. My pastor is a prayer warrior and a true believer in fasting to break through any situation. Also, maybe they should spend some time under the direction of the younger men since they are the ones on fire. Put the younger men on fire in charge of outreaches and evangelism. My pastor would say the Kingdom of God has no seniority: *The last shall be first, and the first shall be last.* Maybe Pastor Jones should come here and do a revival. He'll wake up the dead."

Pastor Franks asked, "Why would you leave such an on fire move of God like that, son?"

"Well, my company appointed me to head up the East Coast operations here. It was a hard decision. I decided I would try it just to get the company back on track. I'm hoping it won't take more than a couple of years," Derek answered, feeling deeply convicted.

Pastor Franks replied, "I thank God he sent you here. I could use a young disciple to look from the outside and tell me what you think. Come to a couple of outreaches with us and show us your secret to win souls."

"Like I said, there are no tricks or gimmicks. Just go up to folks and boldly tell them about Jesus and give your testimony and let God do the rest. Get them to come to a decision right then and there," replied Derek.

"It worked for me," Stuart added. "I got saved right in front of the people who had the most influence over my life. Those guys are probably out to get me, but I don't care. I got Jesus now, and I can handle anything with him in my life."

"Amen," added Pastor Franks. "You used to hang out in the Town Square, didn't you, Stuart? You would mock our teens and laugh at them."

"Yes. I hate to admit it, but I was in that crowd who would go to The Square just to give your church a hard time. We would take your flyers off the doors after you would leave the neighborhood too. I can't wait to go back like the Apostle Paul and show my friends the change Jesus has made in me."

"See. Didn't I tell you he is on fire? I love what God can do in a raw sinner," said Derek.

"This young man is going to do great things for God. He is going to shock this town."

The congregation had prepared a feast for the Andersons. There was fried chicken, ham, potato salad, mashed potatoes, corn on the cob, baked beans, dinner rolls, good old-fashioned lemonade, and a scrumptious chocolate cake prepared by none other than Millie.

The Andersons stayed in town all day. Everyone wanted to have them over. Their calendar was filled for the next two months of Sundays. "I could get to like this," shouted DJ.

"You just like the eating part," Devon returned.

"And did you see the back of the church was full of trees and grass? Next week, I'm bringing extra clothes so I can hang out with some of the other kids and play ball after church," replied DJ.

"Me too," answered Devon. "I bet I can throw farther and run faster than anybody in that whole church!"

"Why don't you two grow up," moaned Daphne. "I'm full and sleepy. Let's see who can be the quietest all the way home." Daphne was asleep in no time. Stuart sat in the back of the SUV reading the Bible the rest of the way home.

CHAPTER 8

A DATE WITH RONNIE

Derek had bought Ronnie her own minivan for transporting the kids back and forth to school and for her running around. School was just a couple weeks away. All the shopping was done. All the school supplies were in the backpacks. "We need to go food shopping for lunches," said Ronnie.

"Any special requests should be made now. I'm only doing this every Friday as usual. You know the program. Make out your lists and give them to me by Thursday."

"I don't care what we get as long as we have plenty of string cheese," answered Devon.

"And juice packs!" added DJ.

"Mom, can I buy lunch at school like the other kids this year?" asked Daphne. "I don't want to look like a fifth grader with a dumb lunch box. It's my senior year. That's embarrassing. It's not like when you went to school, and you carried your little cartoon character lunch boxes. Let me at least get to know everyone before they figure out how much of a dork I am."

"Daphne Lynn Anderson, where I come from that's called being ashamed. You have nothing to be embarrassed about. Of course they will think you are a dork. You and Devon will probably be in a small group of the only ones at school not showing your body piercings, and you'll be wearing pants that cover your thighs."

"They are called capris, Mom, and most girls wear them," answered Daphne.

"Yeah, but yours won't be skin-tight hip huggers, young lady! You are already going to stand out because they will see a difference in you, and people will take notice of that. You have a rare thing. Don't ever lose it. You have the one thing that a girl can never get back once it is lost...innocence, purity, and virginity." Ronnie shouted back at her.

"You think I don't notice how people look at you, guys? You take your innocence and purity for granted. There are girls that have lost that before they are Devon's age and regret it every day. You listen to what I'm saying."

The phone rang. It was Derek. "How about I take my best girl out to lunch today? Meet me at Millie's?" Derek asked.

"Honey, I can't. There is so much to do in the garden. I got laundry and grocery shopping. Can I take a rain check?" she asked.

"I suppose so. I just miss you so much. This office practically runs itself now that I've got my staff on the right track and pointed in the right direction. I have a three o'clock meeting with my staff, and I'm home by five at the latest," answered Derek.

"How 'bout tonight? Just you and me? No kids? We deserve a night out together. I haven't had a moment alone with my wife for almost a month. You've been so busy with the house and getting the kids ready for school. I come home tired and fall asleep on you almost every night. Now that things are going good, I can slow down and enjoy an evening with the love of my life."

"We'll see, honey. It depends on how much I get done today. Thanks for asking though," answered Ronnie.

"I miss you too."

They both hang up the phone. Derek stopped by the florist on the way home and handed Ronnie the most beautiful bouquet of pink and white carnations when he walked in the door.

"Oh, how thoughtful," said Ronnie. "I can't remember the last time you brought me flowers home. Let's see...the last time you bought me flowers and it wasn't Valentine's Day or my birthday was when you wanted to go back to school full time, and you needed me to go back to work...wait a minute... what's going on? What's wrong?" Ronnie asked suspiciously.

"Nothing, baby," laughed Derek as he kissed Ronnie on the forehead. "Can't I bring my beautiful wife a bouquet of flowers just because I'm madly in love with her, and I missed her all day?"

"You're up to something. I'm going to be watching you," replied Ronnie.

Derek had no idea how much Ronnie did today to prepare for tonight. She did the gardening and laundry. She made a quick supper for the kids. They cleaned the kitchen together, and she spent a half hour soaking in the tub with candles lit around her so she could relax.

The girls helped her get all dolled up. "Mom, you and Dad should go out more often. You are so beautiful. I hope I'm this pretty when I get old," stated Devon. "Everyone is going to stop and stare when you walk in the door. Don't you know you have something that a lot of other couples don't? You guys are still in love after all these years. You have not entered the marriage graveyard sitting in front of the TV watching reruns and bringing Dad a beer during the commercials. Dad still looks at you like he just met you, and it's love at first sight. I see the way he looks at you."

"I want my husband to be just like Dad," sighed Daphne. Hearing her girls say that made Ronnie feel so special.

She wore Derek's favorite outfit, her baby blue satin dress that he bought for her birthday last year. Ronnie laid out Derek's dark blue suit that she loved. Derek took a quick shower, and they were out the door. "Behave for your sister. I don't want to hear any bad reports in the morning you two," he warned Devon and DJ as they were exiting.

He held her hand as they walked in the restaurant and opened her door for her all night. Ronnie loved all the special treatment. Derek did those kinds of things all the time, but tonight was different somehow. Derek and Ronnie played little romantic games all night. Whenever they would make eye contact, Ronnie's heart would skip a beat, and she would get butterflies in her stomach when Derek would put his arms around her. It amazed her how he still made her feel that way. They sat together in a cozy booth all romantically instead of across from each other like they usually did. They looked like a couple who was dating instead a couple who had been married for twenty-two years. They went for a walk in The Square after dinner. They felt like they were the only people on the planet. They sat and enjoyed the moonlight and each other's company.

"Hey. What do we want to do for Labor Day?" Ronnie asked.

"How about we drive down to Lake Mystic and check out the company lake house? We could drive down Friday and come home early Saturday evening," answered Derek. "The kids can get the ants out their pants before school starts Tuesday," he added.

"Honey, if I forget to tell you later, thanks for a wonderful evening," said Ronnie. "I needed to get out. Thank you for taking me out and making me feel so special. I bet you don't even know how thankful I am for a husband like you. Spending the rest of my life with you completes everything for me. I can't think of anything else in the world I need besides you and the children. You guys mean everything to me. You know, sometimes I take for granted that I have a loving husband and good kids, and I know I shouldn't. I know that there are people all around us with marriages that are hurting or have children that run away or get into trouble with the police." Ronnie started to cry softly. "Don't cry, honey. This was supposed to be a happy night," said Derek, handing her the hankie out of his suit coat.

"That's why I'm crying. I'm so happy," answered Ronnie. Derek kissed her once more on her forehead and took her hand to stand her up and embraced Ronnie so tenderly. They looked into each other's eyes and smile. As they walked back to the car, Ronnie laid her head on Derek's shoulder.

When they arrived home, DJ and Devon were both asleep on opposite ends of the couch. Daphne was sprawled out on the floor. The monopoly game was all over the coffee table. DJ still had a wad of money in his hands. "Don't worry, honey, I'll make sure they clean all this up in the morning," said Derek. He did not want the evening to end with Ronnie straightening up and getting all tired. Derek carried DJ upstairs and put him to bed. "Either this boy is getting heavy, or I'm getting old," he whispered while looking at Ronnie. "Don't even say it," he added. They both smiled. Ronnie got Devon and Daphne to drag themselves upstairs. She turned off all the lights while Derek checked and rechecked the doors and windows to make sure they were secured for the night.

"I'm turning in. How 'bout you?" Derek asked. They walked upstairs holding hands. Derek and Ronnie shared their first intimate moment in the house that night. Derek whispered softly to Ronnie, "You complete me too." Ronnie slept so soundly in Derek's arms the rest of the night.

CHAPTER 9

THE LAKE MYSTIC MONSTER

Labor Day weekend had finally arrived. Ronnie and the kids spent the morning shopping for food for the outing and school lunches. They also found a store in The Square that sold lake toys and swimwear. Everything was set. They all waited for Derek to come home from work. Derek planned a half-day at the office and told everyone to have a safe weekend and to come back Tuesday refreshed and ready to work. When Derek arrived at the house, the kids and Ronnie anxiously packed up the SUV, and they were on their way to Lake Mystic. It was a scenic drive. They were there in less than an hour. The lake house was rustic and had a certain charm to it. There was a deck out back with a barbecue area and several tables with huge colorful umbrellas and matching lawn chairs. This lake house was for company retreats and teamwork seminars. There was a hiking path out back with a bike trail. There were beautiful trees and shrubs surrounding it that gave it ample shade. It had three stories. The first floor had a large game room with a pool table, an air hockey table, and a ping pong table. Set up in the corner was a full-stocked wet bar, and to the right of it was a small room with a wide-screen television with lots of cushy furniture, and that room led to another room that had a computer center with four private computer stations set up. There was also an entertainment center with stereo components and what looked like a dance floor in a room adjacent to the computer center. Every room was soundproof.

"Looks like they did some partying out here," said Derek, as he walked throughout in amazement. The hardwood floor was all dark wood. The walls gave the appearance of a log lake house. There was a huge fireplace as you walked to the rear of the first floor. There were a couple of sofas and large pillows on the floor of that room. As you walked more to the rear of it, you had to step up to the kitchen area. It was furnished with state-of-the-art stainless steel appliances. There was a walk-in refrigerator, a large pantry, and a little cubby off to the right with four sets of washers and dryers. The kitchen was full of lake houses and shelves that matched the floor. There were navy and beige gingham curtains that gave everything a country charm. There was a large banquet-type room with eight large tables that each had twelve chairs. The chair pads and tablecloths matched the kitchen curtains.

"Now, this is my kind of kitchen," said Ronnie, although it's big enough for Paul Bunyan and his family," she added. That was the second floor.

There were two master bedrooms and three large bedrooms on the third floor. The first master bedroom had French-type doors with an enclosed balcony that overlooked the lake. "We'll take this one," agreed Ronnie and Derek. There was a sunken tub that looked like a small wading pool in the bathroom and a mini sauna. The room was decorated with a country patchwork quilt and had a workstation with a computer in it.

"I hope you don't think you are going to be doing any work in this bedroom. Lock your briefcase and cell phone in the car," said Ronnie. "Better yet, give them to me."

"Not a chance," answered Derek, "this is *our* weekend. I didn't even bring my briefcase to the lake."

"I've trained you well," replied Ronnie.

The other master bedroom was on the opposite end of the lake house, and it overlooked the woods. It had pretty much the same décor, but the room didn't have a workstation. None of the kids wanted that room. "It looks kinda spooky," said Devon.

"It will give me nightmares all weekend," said DJ.

"DJ and I are going to get the grill started, and we'll leave the unpacking to the ladies. Let's go, little man!" Derek shouted.

Ronnie and the girls unpacked the food and put away the clothes. "If we had known about this place, we could have come here sooner," said Ronnie. "Your dad just found out about it last week. We'll probably spend the holidays here. It's a nice place to get away from what little city life Mystic has," she added.

"I'd like to have a sleepover out here in the fall, like Octoberish, and sit around and tell scary stories," said Devon. "Now I can't wait until school starts on Tuesday so I can make some new friends."

"Mom, wouldn't it be neat to have a Halloween costume party out here for Dad's work?" Daphne asked.

"I'd help you. We can decorate the place with carved pumpkins and landscape the front like an old graveyard. It will be a good way to get to know all of Dad's employees and their families, and they could invite their new clients."

"That's a super idea, Daphne," answered Ronnie. "I'll talk it over with your father tonight," she added.

"The coals are ready. Where's the meat?" asked Derek.

"It's right here!" Ronnie yelled back. They had rib eye steaks and corn ready to go on the grill. Ronnie put some steak fries in the oven, and the girls tossed a salad. Dinner was fantastic. There weren't any leftovers.

"Who's ready to lose at Scrabble?" asked Derek.

"You are, Dad, unless you plan on cheating again. The words you make up are not words. Did you bring a dictionary this time?" asked Daphne. Derek played Scrabble with Devon and DJ for an hour while Ronnie and Daphne cleared the table and cleaned the kitchen.

"Can we go swimming tomorrow?" asked Daphne.

"Of course," Ronnie answered. "We are going to spend most of the day at the lake. I'm going to pack us a lunch, and DJ and Devon will bury your father in the sand like they always did back home." Ronnie and Daphne both get a little homesick. There is silence.

"Daphne, I want you to know I meant what I said about this school year. I don't plan it to be any different than school was back home. I expect you girls to make lots of friends but don't forget to share your salvation with them. So many people don't know the first thing about why Jesus died on the cross. That's our job to get the word out. Your testimony is expected. It's something you can't keep to yourself. I'm sure Mystic High School has just as many hurting teenagers as Bradley did," Ronnie said sincerely.

"OK, Mom. I promise I will share my testimony. I've got Devon and Stuart for backup," Daphne answered.

Game time was over, and everyone was getting tired. "I guess we'd better go to bed. We have a big day planned for tomorrow," said Derek. "We are going to spend the entire day at the lake, take a nap, and then we'll drive home around six o'clock so we can be all rested up for church."

Surrounded by woods, the lake house was very dark at night. Devon and DJ decided to bunk together. Daphne put on her headphones and listened to music until she fell asleep. Ronnie and Derek stayed up talking for a little while, made love then drifted off to sleep. At approximately 12:10 a.m., there was a loud thud on the front porch. Derek jumped up and got his handgun.

"Honey, I didn't know you brought your gun, but I'm glad you did. Be careful," said Ronnie.

"Stay upstairs," answered Derek. Devon and DJ were in their parents' room and had jumped in the bed with Ronnie, hiding under the covers.

"Is it the Loch Ness Monster or Big Foot?" DJ asked.

"No, more like the Lake Mystic Monster," Devon answered from under the covers. "The Loch Ness Monster is over in Paris or Ireland or somewhere like Japan," she added.

"Please read a book soon, honey." Ronnie laughed. "It's in Scotland."

Meanwhile downstairs, Derek stood at the front door and peeped through the peephole. He heard the front door knob jiggling. "I have a loaded gun in my hand, so I don't suggest you open that door!" Derek yelled.

"It's me, Mr. Anderson. Charity. I … I … m … m…mean Ms. Foster. Don't shoot."

"Charity, what are you doing here at this lake house?" Derek asked angrily. "This is company property, and you did not clear it with me."

"Roger and I used to come here for the weekend all the time. He gave me a spare key and told me I could use the place whenever I wanted," Charity answered.

"Roger is not your boss anymore. You do not have the authority to be here," Derek replied sternly. Just then, a tall slender gentleman walked up on the porch and asked Charity where did she want the rest of the baggage. "Excuse me, Charity, but who is this?" Derek asked.

"Th…Th…This is my fr…fr…friend, Donald Richardson. We were planning to come to the lake for the weekend, and you know, get away and relax," Charity answered.

"I'm sorry, but my family is here. You and Donald can stay tonight, but you are leaving first thing in the morning. You'll be staying in separate bedrooms upstairs. I'll have Ronnie move my son's things out of the room for Donald. I will not have you sleeping around and carrying on under the same roof with my children here. We *will* discuss this Tuesday, Charity," Derek replied.

Donald said to Derek, "Look you Stone Age freak! This is the millennium. Where have you been—buried under a rock or something? Come on, Charity. We can get a motel up the road. I didn't drive all the way down here to sleep in separate rooms. I came to have some fun like we always do. Go call and see if there are any vacancies." Charity called a couple of lakeside motels.

"There are no vacancies, Donald. I guess we will have to take those separate rooms after all," she replied nervously.

"I would rather sleep in my truck than be in here with this cave man. Are you coming or not?" Donald demanded.

"I think I will stay in here. I don't like to be around you when you're mad especially when you've been drinking," Charity answered.

"Suit yourself," said Donald, storming out of the front door of the lake house slamming it behind him.

"I'm really sorry, Mr. Anderson. I didn't mean to interrupt your family outing. I am so ashamed and embarrassed. I can imagine what your family will think of me," added Charity. Just then, Ronnie came downstairs.

"How about I make us some coffee, Charity? Feel like some girl talk?" she asked.

"Let's go in this bowling alley they call a kitchen." Derek nodded at Ronnie in approval. "I think I'll go check on the kids."

As Ronnie prepared the coffee, Charity was sitting at the counter with her head down, silently sobbing. She felt so ashamed she couldn't even look at her. "Mrs. Anderson, I don't want you to get the impression that I sleep around like this all the time. I'm so lonely and afraid to be alone. I don't know why I drink so much lately. Can you ever forgive me for intruding on your family?" Charity asked.

"Of course, I forgive you. Let me tell you a story about another lonely girl. I used to be so lonely and alone just like you. But no one wanted to be around me because I always had this chip on my shoulder. I blamed everyone else for my failures and mistakes. Nothing was ever my fault. I wanted to blame my father for all of my unhappiness because he had abandoned my mother. What I failed to realize was that my mother drove him away with all *her* complaining and pity parties. I was beginning to turn into my mother. I never had anything nice to say about anything. I hated men. I hated the world. Then one day, I stopped and looked at myself in the mirror, and I didn't like what I saw. I saw this selfish, bitter person with an unnecessary need for attention, and I took a good look at how pitiful I was, and I couldn't look at myself in that mirror. I was a wreck. My whole countenance was this angry bitter look all over my face. I was introverting myself away from the world. I wouldn't let anyone get close to me or get to know me. I didn't trust anyone. But one day, I was studying on the campus lawn, and I saw Derek walking around inviting people out to his Bible study, and I was so mean to him. I told him to get away from me with that 'Jesus crap.' I was fine like I was, and I didn't need him telling me what I needed. Well, thank God, Derek did not give up on me. He would always speak to me and treat me with so much respect. I started noticing how happy he seemed and what a good attitude he had about life. I wanted that joy and peace of mind that he had. I started sitting in on his Bible study sessions he had in the student union. At first, I would only stay for about ten minutes, but then I started staying a little longer and really listening to what he had to say. One night, he asked me and some of my 'associates' (making quotation marks with her fingers). Oh, remember? I didn't dare call anyone *my* friend back then. Anyway, he asked a few of us if we wanted to go out for coffee. He said we would all go out as a group. He was not trying to hit on anyone, and he was not looking for a date. At first, I thought he was gay or something because I never saw him with a girl. What I discovered though was that he was not looking for a girlfriend but a wife, and she had to be serving God. He told us that he was born again and had given his life to Jesus, and he was not going to wreck his testimony on empty relationships. I would watch him around other females, and he was always a gentleman. He would never be put in a compromising position, and whenever we went anywhere together, it was always in a group setting. Well, one day on campus, Derek did his usual altar call, and I finally responded. Charity, it was like a big weight was lifted off me. I couldn't find that big chip that was on my shoulders anymore. I started genuinely caring about others instead of my so-called problems, which weren't even problems. I started sharing my testimony with others. At this point, I still had no interest in Derek. I was so messed up that I had to get my personal relationship with Jesus Christ on the right track before I could even think about sharing any part of my life with anyone else. How could I love anyone if I didn't love myself? I kept going to church and school and working part time to keep myself on track. God kept opening doors of opportunity. My grades got better, and I got a full scholarship and did not even have to work the last two years of school. That was such a blessing because I could attend church and school full time and not have the conflict of a job whenever we had special events going on. God kept revealing himself to me and becoming more and more real in my life. I kept studying and reading his word and praying and sharing my testimony with other people on campus.

"Well, about a year and a half later, Derek asked our pastor and his wife about me and what kind of Christian did they think I was. He knew he was ready to get married. My pastor and his wife asked me out to dinner, and it just so happened that Derek was also there that night. I really didn't think anything of it until the pastor's wife asked me how I felt about marriage. What my plans were for the future—blah, blah, blah—and questioning me about was I going to be a career woman, and if I wanted to be a wife and mom someday—right in the middle of dinner putting me on the spot and everything. Well, Derek was sitting there just eating up every word I would say. I told her I wanted to finish my degree in education, but I definitely wanted to get married now that I had Jesus in my heart, and I felt I could truly love someone besides myself, and that I didn't have the hate in my heart for men anymore, and I had written my father a letter a year ago and had forgiven him and asked him to also forgive me. So then my pastor just bluntly jumps in and asks me what kind of man did I want to marry? I gave him the favorite text book answer: I want to marry a solid Christian who was on fire for God and certain about wanting to serve God. Derek was sitting right at the table, and I was so embarrassed, but I admitted in front of everyone that I hoped that I could find a man like Derek because he loved God and was not ashamed of the Gospel, and he would make some woman a happy wife. Well, my pastor and his wife 'conveniently' left the room and just left me and Derek sitting at the table like they were going to get dessert or coffee or something, and Derek just comes out and told me that he admired how I carried myself as a Christian, and he said he knew that I had one more semester left, and he wanted to know if when I graduated if I wanted to be a career woman or would I be interested in getting married and starting a family, like he hadn't heard what the pastor's wife had just asked me two minutes ago (Ronnie said, turning cupping her hands around her mouth), because his plan after graduation was to get married and have a bunch of kids and be this computer expert or engineering executive and all this stuff. He had already had a lot of job offers because he had done some independent contracting, but he also still had one semester left of school. So I asked him, 'Married to whom?'

Derek said, 'To me.' He pulled out this teeny diamond engagement ring. I was speechless. So I paused for a moment and said, 'Well, I have to talk this over with God and my pastor," and I started getting flustered, but I was so flattered. I couldn't even look at Derek the rest of the evening.

"I started praying to God that if Derek was the husband he wanted me to have let me not go on feelings because I am lonely. Let me know in my heart that he is the one. If he is not living clean, please reveal it and not let my heart be broken again. So after six months of 'group dating,' I mean we never put ourselves in a situation where we were alone. That would be too tempting, and it would wreck both our testimonies equally because who knew how many countless other young converts, and new converts were watching us as an example. After six more months, my pastor announced that Derek and I were getting married June 1 during the Sunday morning service. Some people did not even know that Derek and I were even seeing each other, not because we were sneaking around, but because we never displayed any affection in public, and we were not going off alone. He would call me every day, and we would pray together and have lunch together most days with our friends, but still, like I said, we were very discreet, respectful to one another, and righteous. The day finally came for us to get married, and I knew nothing about being a wife. I had no example except for the couples in my church. My parents fought all the time, and my mom was so cold to my dad that I never saw any love between them. I really didn't know how to love Derek. I asked the pastor's wife a lot of questions. She told me to put God first in our marriage, and we would find out the best plan for our marriage through his direction. She said it just gets better year after year. She was honest enough to tell me there would be ups and downs and highs and lows. There will be times when we won't be able to stand each other but stick it out because marriage is forever. No one could do it for us. Leave our parents out of it. Never go home crying to Mother and never take advice from any other women in the church married or unmarried unless it was on cleaning and cooking tips, and we would be fine. On my wedding day, I must've thrown up a dozen times. My stomach was so nervous. I was trying to act like I was so brave and had everything under control. My dad shows up at the wedding drunk and disgusting. He was mad because we weren't going to serve any liquor. He fell asleep in his car. One of the brothers in the church gave me away. My mother spent the whole day trashing my dad in front of the congregation talking about how he was no good and how he had left her with three children, and she nagged and nagged the whole day. It still was the one of the happiest days of my life besides the day I gave my life to Jesus and the birth of my children. I cannot imagine my life without Derek now. We've been together for twenty-two years. It's amazing what God can do. Derek and I are a miracle. We both come from broken homes. We didn't know anything about love or how to love and look what the Lord has done in our lives."

Charity looked up at Ronnie and asked, "How can I have the joy and happiness that you speak about? I've been married twice, and it never worked. God couldn't possibly have a plan for my life. I have been such a horrible person. You don't know the things I have done. You can't even imagine the men that I have manipulated and the humiliating things that I have done before God. How could he ever forgive someone like me?"

Ronnie answered, "God loves you, Charity. He just hates your sin. You can say a sinner's prayer tonight and have a clean slate like a newborn child. Everything you've ever done will be forgotten the very instant you say this prayer. God throws it into the sea of forgetfulness. Would you like to pray with me now?" Charity and Ronnie said a sinner's prayer. Ronnie had Charity break curses of lust and immorality and bind the spirit of rejection.

Charity told Ronnie, "I know what you mean now about the weight being lifted off of you. I never imagined that God could love me so much or that he could ever forgive me. Thank you so much for sharing the Gospel and praying with me." Ronnie and Charity hugged. They all went back to bed.

When the Andersons woke up, Charity and Donald were gone. Charity left a note in the kitchen that read: "Dear Anderson family. I would like to apologize for the conduct of Donald and myself last night. We have left for the city. Hope this note finds you in

God's love and care. Looking forward to having that talk with you on Tuesday morning, Mr. Anderson. I accept whatever discipline you feel I deserve. Enjoy the rest of your weekend and have a safe trip home. Charity."

Derek asked Ronnie, "What did you guys talk about? Charity seems so mellowed out."

"I shared my testimony with her, told her that Jesus could love even her, and led her through the sinner's prayer. Sounds like she got a good night's sleep too."

The Andersons spend the day at the lake and put the lake house back in order and headed back to the city. The kids slept almost all the way home.

The children were all excited about starting school. After church, they made sure everything was ready for Tuesday. Monday would be the last day of freedom in the Anderson home. Sunday was the last night to stay up late. Derek and Ronnie took school very seriously. Homework was a priority. Although the children had been helping out Aunt Millie at the lodge, it was time to buckle up. Ronnie and Derek explained to her that they would only be able to help on Saturday after outreach which she understood and agreed.

The leaves were starting to turn beautiful colors. All the beautiful colors of fall were coming out. Ronnie never imagined Mystic was such a beautiful city. Her garden was thrusting out the last of its fruits and vegetables. Too bad Derek's promotion was so late in the year.

"There will always be next season," she thought to herself.

CHAPTER 10

SCHOOL DAZE

The first day of school was going to be hectic. "Let's see, I've got to get Daphne and Devon off to the high school, take DJ to school and get my name on the list for the PTA, go to the quickie mart, go to the office supply store to get paper so I can get cranking on my newsletter. Won't the girls in Bradley be surprised to finally hear from me?" Ronnie thought out loud.

"Do you need me for anything, honey?" Derek asked. "This is your last chance. I could go in later, and we could celebrate the kids getting out the house," he said, raising his eyebrows.

"I'll take a rain check today. I've got a ton of stuff to do. You know how I like to go in on the first day and let the staff know I'm available where ever I'm needed," Ronnie answered.

"Once a teacher always a teacher," replied Derek, shaking his head as he left the house.

Devon and Daphne were pretty excited about meeting new friends. They got along well, but Devon wanted to meet girls that liked sports just like her. Ronnie expected her to go out for basketball as soon as the tryouts would be posted. Daphne would probably try out for cheerleading or pep club or something like that. The girls were totally opposite, and their parents found it hard to believe that they could get along so well.

When Ronnie and DJ arrived at Glenridge Elementary School, Mrs. Taylor, the assistant principal, was standing out front greeting all the students and parents. "Good morning, Mrs. Anderson, this must be your son Derek. We are so glad to have him at our school. School is out at 3:12 p.m. Have a good day."

Ronnie replied, "I was planning to come in today and be a help mom like I did in the Bradley Elementary School back in Ohio. Have they started sign-ups for PTA? Can I browse through the library? I was planning to stay and have lunch with DJ on his first day."

"Mrs. Anderson, your son is in the fifth grade. Don't you think it would look a little strange if you tagged along all day with him?" Mrs. Taylor asked.

"I wasn't going to tag along with him. I wanted to stay and get to know the staff and help out. I used to teach third grade for five years," Ronnie answered.

"Don't you have something to do at home or maybe some shopping you'd like to catch up on?" asked one of the teachers.

"Well, actually, I do have shopping to do, but that can wait. Getting to know my child's school is more important to me right now. I was only planning to stay a couple of hours."

"Very well," Principal Taylor replied, walking away.

There were children scurrying everywhere. There were little kindergartners clinging tightly on their mother's clothes. There were younger siblings crying because they wanted to stay with their older brother or sister. The kindergarten teacher, Miss Fields, looked helpless. Ronnie went right up to her and asked if she wanted some help calming the kids down.

"I could read them a story, or we could sing a song."

"Who are you?" asked one of the mothers. "Are you a teacher?"

"I used to be a third grade teacher," replied Ronnie. My husband and I decided that it would benefit our family most if I stayed home."

"Oh no, not another Bible thumper!" shouted one of the moms. "I guess you want to run the PTA and ban all the harmless fun books on magic and fairy tales and spoil all the kids' fun?"

"I do intend to be in on the PTA, but I don't plan to spoil anyone's fun. I'm here to make sure that the wrong materials are not being distributed amongst our children. They have enough to be scared of instead of us filling their heads with scary stories and magnifying witchcraft," Ronnie replied.

"If you wanted to stay at home, why are you hanging around here?" one of the parents named Tammy asked.

"Look, I'm offering my help in any way you need me. I will be in the office," Ronnie answered.

"Wait, said Miss Fields. "I could surely use your help. This is my first year at this school. I'm excited and nervous just like the children. I would love to have you stay and help out." She explained to Ronnie how she just moved to Mystic from Boston. Her fiancé is a salesman, and she wanted to be closer to him so they could finally get married. He'd been promising her for two years that they'd get married. "I've finally put my foot down and moved out here. I'm tired of our long distance relationship," she added.

Tammy interrupted, "Marriage ain't all it's cracked up to be, honey. My husband works all day, comes home and plops down on the sofa and drinks beers and watches TV all night like me, and the kids don't exist. You'll see, once he pumps you up with a couple of babies, he'll start ignoring you and treating you like you were his personal maid. Don't gain a few pounds after having kids either. He'll start staring at all these other women right in front of you and calling you names like fat cow and thunder thighs." All the other mothers agree with her.

Ronnie thought to herself, "I've got to be here every day. These women need Jesus in their lives quick. They are miserable. Their marriages are hurting. They are bitter. They have no hope."

Ronnie helped Miss Fields put nametags on every kid and got the school supplies lists ready. It felt like she was teaching again. She helped Miss Fields make a bulletin board with all the children's birth dates on it. They sang songs and said the Pledge of Allegiance. Ronnie helped show the frightened children how to go to the girls and boys bathrooms. Miss Fields was really happy she stayed.

It was after 11:00 o'clock and almost time for morning kinder-garten to end. Ronnie said her good-byes to the children and headed for the front door. DJ was on his way to art class. She gave him a nice big hug and told him she would see him at 3:15 sharp. DJ was really glad his mom did not stay for lunch. He had already made two friends in class and didn't know how to break the news to her that he wanted to eat with them. Ronnie already knew and did not want to interrupt his getting to know his new friends.

Ronnie did the shopping at both stores, and it was time to pick up the girls at the high school. "Mom!" Devon shouted. "I made the most baskets at lunchtime. I bet I can whip anybody in this school at basketball."

"Showing off again?" asked Ronnie.

"Nope, just putting it out there so they'll recognize. I even held back because I can't let them see all my moves before tryouts. I've got two weeks to brush up on my long shot," Devon answered.

Daphne came walking to the car with Stuart. "Hi, Mrs. Anderson," said Stuart. "I showed Daphne and Devon around today and introduced them to some of my straight friends. Cameron was being a real jerk today, but I ignored him. Now he wants to fight me and stuff. I told him I would pray for him."

"Good for you, Stuart," said Ronnie. "Are you busy tonight? Want to come for dinner? I make a mean meatloaf."

"I'd really like that. Thanks. I don't get home-cooked meals very often," replied Stuart. "I'll come by as soon as I get my homework done. Listen to me. I *never* used to do homework. I think I'm going to like school this year. For once, I will be in class and not ditching in the bathrooms or pulling the fire alarm when its test time. That was my specialty. It felt weird not being high in class. The teachers actually made sense to me. I used to disrupt class and laugh and tell stupid disgusting jokes until I'd get sent to the office. Then I'd just ditch with my friends."

"You *are* a miracle, Stuart," said Daphne. "I remember the night we met at the pizza place. You made a terrible impression on me. You are 100 percent changed. I couldn't stand you. You were the type of kid I loathed. Now we are good friends. My dad is crazy about you. Sure, he loves DJ, but you're the older son he's been waiting for. DJ is still kinda young to do a lot of things. He is going to be taking you everywhere. Be prepared. Don't be late for dinner!" she yelled as they drop Stuart off at home.

Ronnie and the girls arrived at DJ's school where he was waiting out front with two kids. "Mom, I have six new best friends, I like my teacher, I like the playground, I like my desk!" DJ screamed.

"That's good," answered Ronnie. "You'll be seeing a lot of me there, so be on your best behavior, son."

"I promise," said DJ.

That night at dinner, everyone was so full of conversation except for Stuart. "Don't you like my meatloaf?" Ronnie asked.

"It's great, Mrs. Anderson. I was just thinking about when I leave here. I'll be going home to an empty house. You guys have so much love here. I have nothing to go home to—"

Derek interrupted, "Let me tell you something, young man. God did not save you for you to be all sad and unhappy. Continue to show your family the change in you so they will notice the difference in your life, and it will affect theirs. Pray against everything unclean going on in your home and have nothing to do with any of it. Don't stop reading your Bible and pray before you start your day during the day and at night before you go to bed. Pray like I showed you. Be bold and strong with it and believe God to break through. Most importantly, wait on God. Don't give up."

Stuart smiled at Derek. "You can always make me feel better, sir. You always know what to say."

Derek answered, "That's another thing, Stuart. You can call me Derek. We're friends, right?"

"Right," Stuart answered.

Derek, Stuart and DJ teamed up and beat the girls at Pictionary. It was 8:00 p.m. and time for DJ to get ready for bed. "I better start heading home too," said Stuart. Derek offered to drive Stuart home. He only lived six blocks from the Andersons, but Derek loved spending time with his new convert, besides he was worried about Cameron and his friends trying to catch Stuart off guard and alone at night.

All the way there, they talked about Cameron and how he was threatened by Cameron's little gang of thugs at school today. Derek suggested he avoid all confrontations with them but stand his ground if he had to. Derek told him to never let himself be caught alone with them or get cornered. They will fight him dirty that way. He told Stuart that if Cameron wanted to fight him one-on-one, so be it, but don't provoke a fight with him. "Cameron just has to prove to his friends that he is tough right now. He's really hurt that you are not marching to his tune anymore. He probably is jealous because you have a better future than he does. Keep praying, and he will come around. When you get a moment alone with him, share the Gospel. See if you can get him to say a sinner's prayer like you did," Derek suggested.

"Cameron is too stubborn and prideful. He has this image to uphold. He wants all the girls to think he is Don Juan, and he tries to be tough like "The Godfather," Stuart answered. If he orders you to do something, and you don't do it, the gang will get you bad. If he wants you to be in his gang and you say no, he will have his *Mystic Mafia* hurt you. We stabbed a boy in the leg once who didn't want to join our gang. We broke all the windows in their home and set their deck furniture on fire. They moved away within a week. The police are afraid of us. When they would see us walking, they would turn down the next block to avoid us. Mr. Anderson, I mean Derek, you don't realize what kind of monster I used to be. I have vandalized and terrorized the citizens of this town for the past two years. How can anyone in this town believe I have changed?" Stuart asked.

"By not hanging around the Mystic Mafia first of all," Derek answered. "Refer to them as *they* and not *we*. You no longer belong to that nonsense. You could offer to do yardwork or something to right the wrong you have done to your neighbors. Better yet, Stuart, can you drive? I need a runner in the afternoons, and we have a company van, and I could use a courier to make deliveries for me. It pays $10 an hour for about three hours a day. It's not much, but it will put some money in your pocket and keep you out of harm's way. Plus, it will show the Mystic residents that you can be trusted, and they will see the change in you."

"Yes, I can drive. I got my license two years ago. You would trust me with such important stuff?" he asked.

"Stuart, are you a Christian? Are you changed? Don't you want someone to believe in you? I have faith in you. I trust you," Derek answered. Stuart was so overwhelmed.

"I wish I had a father like you," Stuart replied.

"You have something better. You have Jesus Christ. He's a father to the fatherless," Derek added. "You can start Monday, and you just take the van to school, and you can drive over afterwards and pick up your deliveries and keep the van for transportation. I will make sure it is filled up for you every weekend to make your deliveries all week. You have to replace whatever gas you use for personal use. We'll drive over to my job on Saturday and pick up the van after outreach. Deal?"

"Deal," Stuart answered proudly.

CHAPTER 11

HALLOWEEN TOWN

It was finally October and time to decorate for Halloween. The Andersons were decorating their home like a cemetery with tombstones in the front lawn.

"This is my favoritest time of year," said Daphne.

"*Most* favorite," corrected Ronnie.

"Anyways…from Halloween to Christmas I'm the *most* happiest," added Daphne smiling at her mom.

Stuart came by to lend a hand in the decorating. Derek had three witches being hung from a tree in the front lawn. "Honey, don't you think we are going a little over the edge?" Ronnie asked.

"No. I mock witches. They mock my Jesus, so I can mock them. They want to flaunt their satanic religion? I will show this town what Jesus Christ says about witchcraft," Derek answered.

Two days later, a note is placed on the Anderson door. "Please remove your disgusting display or else." Derek left his display in the yard. "They don't scare me," he said. "If he was a real man, he would've signed his name on the note or knocked on my door."

It's the weekend of the party at the lake house, and the Andersons drive down early to decorate and wait for the caterers. "This is going to be the party of all parties," said Ronnie. Millie had trays delivered with submarine sand 'witches,' wings, potato chips, a chocolate dessert she and Ronnie made with devil's food cake, gummy worms, and chocolate-whipped topping. They took miniature dolls and made a gravesite with gummy bugs coming crawling all over the bodies. They used graham crackers with RIP written across them for the headstones. Wicked awesome. The punch bowl had a large hand hanging out of it. When you rang the doorbell, it screamed.

Derek had some lunch gift cards and gift baskets for costume prizes, and the grand prize was a weekend in Boston at the Hilton for the best costume. The costumes were spectacular. They were judged for scariest, funniest, and most original.

DJ and Stuart helped pick up all night so there wouldn't be too much to clean up later. The girls made sure the bathrooms stayed tidy so their mom could concentrate on their guests. There was just finger foods, punch, coffee, and dessert, but everyone had a great time. This was such a great way to get to know Derek's coworkers and their families. Miss Fields, the kindergarten teacher, was there. It just so happened that one of Derek's sales reps, Mike Roper, was her fiancé. What a small world.

Derek announced that night that sales productivity was at an all-time high, and he was putting together something for his crew and their families for Thanksgiving or early December. He told everyone to keep their calendars open if possible. He announced that he was promoting a couple of the sales reps to senior sales reps and increasing their commissions. Mike was one of the promoted reps.

The party ended at ten. Derek offered anyone who wanted to stay over the two extra rooms. They also had cots delivered from The Lighthouse Lodge along with bedding. DJ and Stuart would bunk together as well as Devon and Daphne. Mostly everyone decided to drive home except for a handful. Ronnie, Millie, and Derek provided breakfast to those who stayed. The Andersons drove home Saturday afternoon to find their home had been egged, and their display had been torn down. There was fertilizer smeared all over the display and the front of the house. Derek was not surprised nor was he angry. He called a cleaning service to help them clean up the mess. There was a note on the door this time that read: "You went a little too far with the display. I asked you nicely to take it down. Next time, I won't be so nice."

Derek said, "Wait till they see what I have in store for Christmas."

Ronnie asked, "What are you up to, honey?"

"I don't know," answered Derek, "but I've got plenty of time to plan."

CHAPTER 12

THE MOB SQUAD

Stuart was driving the van through the Town Square making his deliveries as usual when all of a sudden, the Mystic Mafia shows up. "Where'd you get them wheels, man? You work now? I thought I taught you to take what you want. You're making me look bad, Stu," Cameron replied.

"I'm not a part of the Mystic Mafia anymore. I gave my life to Jesus, and I work for a living," Stuart answered. "I don't take from anybody. I've changed. Jesus can change you guys too if you let him in your hearts."

Cameron got in his face. "You better be glad I like you, or you would have a knife in your heart for turning your back on the family," he added.

"If you want to fight me, Cameron, that's fine. I'll only fight you. It has to be a fair fight. I am not afraid of you. Put your knives and cowardly weapons away. I will fight you right here, and we can get this over with," Stuart answered.

"No, I'm a lover not a fighter. I let my boys handle my light work," Cameron replied.

"You know what, Cameron?" Stuart asked. "You guys are all cowards. That's why you travel in a gang. You are probably scared of the dark too. Don't you ever wonder what it would be like to just be yourself and not have to put up the fronts? I'm praying for you guys. I pray that Jesus Christ not let you have one moment's rest until you give your life to him. I pray that your life will be so unfulfilled until you turn it over to him. Aren't you tired of using girls and pretending to be some fake Don Juan? Why can't you have just one girl friend or better yet quit ruining the lives of what decent girls we have left in this town?"

"I won't stop until I have your 'new daddy's' precious girls. That's what I want—fresh meat. What's the matter, Stu? You not getting any? Daddy got the chastity belt on? You are so not cool anymore! We could've run this town together! But no! You had to go get religious on me!" Cameron yelled.

"Cameron, come take a ride with me without 'your boys,' Stuart said. "Let me tell you how Jesus has changed my life. If I can just get you by yourself, I could talk to you. When you are with them, you have to prove you're tough. Come with me, and I will tell you all about Jesus and how he has turned my life around. You, of all people, know I used to be no good. You know how many girls' lives I have destroyed by taking away their innocence. Aren't you the least bit curious about how *I* can change so radically? I'm a walking, talking miracle. Look at me! You, of all people, know the person I used to be. I have not cursed at you one time. I have nothing but love and respect for you. Maybe if you give your life to Jesus, these idiot followers of yours will too. Aren't you tired of living like this? This town hated me. Now they see a change in me, and I have respect again. I'm even paying back all the damages *we* have done in this town. I am getting good grades because I am doing homework. I do extra credit so I can hopefully graduate this year. I can play sports this year too, if I chose to because I have a good attendance record and because of my grades. Do you think Derek would trust me with this van if he didn't think I was changed? He's only known me for a few months and look at the responsibility he has trusted me with."

Cameron told the guys to meet at his house in one hour. He got in the van with Stuart. "You got thirty minutes to 'change' me. If I don't give my life to your Jesus, you have to get back in the family. Deal?" Cameron asked.

"No deal," said Stuart. "Whether or not you give your life to Jesus is up to you. I will not trade my salvation for my old life. Why would I want to be cleansed by the blood of Jesus and then put that old scum back on me? You know how we all became blood brothers? Let me tell you about the blood of Jesus. One precious drop of his blood is more powerful than anything on this Earth. It can heal the sick, restore a marriage and change a no-good thug like me into a useful human being. It can take away your addiction to alcohol and drugs. It will cleanse your mind, body, and soul. When you give your life to Jesus, you are a new creature. You don't want to be the same. A weight is lifted from you. I can't explain it, but I know how *I* feel. It gave me courage to face you guys today. With Jesus Christ, I fear nothing. Because if you guys did stab me, I know I am going to heaven. If you die, Cameron, where will you go? Do you really want to go to hell? Remember the night I surrendered my life to Jesus? Derek asked you that question and you pridefully said, 'To hell with my granddad, dad, and brother.' Is that where you want to go? You do realize that after this life is your true eternity, which means forever, so if you go to hell, it is forever. So what do you say? You want to give your life to Jesus and be forgiven of your sins and have a fresh start?"

"That's all sounds so great, Stu. I do see the change in you, but I'm too young to think about giving up on a lifetime of fun. Maybe when I'm around thirty; I just can't do it right now. I don't have someone like Derek like you do. Don't give up on me, man. I hope you will still be my friend. I'm just not ready yet. I can't make a decision that big yet. I'm only seventeen years old," answered Cameron.

"I am going to ask you this same question every day until you change your mind. You're wrong about Derek. He likes you—he just hates to see you guys throw your lives away. He used to be just like us, didn't care about school, getting high, drinking, robbing people, using girls the whole nine yards. That's why he can relate to us. He knows exactly where we are coming from because he has been there," said Stuart. "I got something for you to read. You can hide it from the guys if you are ashamed for them to see you with it. It is a book Derek gave me on how a born-again teenager is just like a born-again adult. It is eye opening. We think we are too young to give up fun, but the truth is we are not too young to go to hell."

Cameron saw his friends coming toward his house. He hid the Bible under his coat. "I gotta go," said Stuart. "I'll see ya at school tomorrow or around. Cameron, don't forget what I said. Anytime you want to pray, let me know. You know I'll always be your friend, but we can't hang around together as long as you live life the way you do because the Bible says to not be unequally yoked. It means that you witness to those that are lost, but you do not follow their path even if they are your friends or family." Stuart pulled off and drove home to do his homework.

That night, Stuart started to pray for Cameron. "Lord, I pray that Cameron will turn his life around before it is too late. Let my life be an example for him so that he can be an example for others. I pray that he won't wait too long. Give me the words to say to him that will break through his heart of stone. I know he has been hurt and has no male example in his life. Let Derek and me become that example for him. Let me also be an example for Mom and Grandma. I bind all witchcraft and evil speaking and sorcery from this house. I lose the Holy Spirit in this house and no other. Amen."

A little after midnight, the Anderson's phone rang.

"Hello?" answered Derek in a groggy voice. "It's me, Stuart. I apologize for disturbing your family at this hour, but Cameron's been shot. His mom just called me from the hospital. She said he kept asking for the two of us all the way to the hospital. He's in surgery right now. We need to go over and pray for him!" Stuart said with excitement in his voice.

"I'll be right over to pick you up," Derek answered.

"What's wrong, honey?" Ronnie asked. "Remember the kid who gave Stuart such a hard time at the pizza place? He's been shot. He's in surgery. Stuart and I are going over to pray for him and for his family."

"I'll start praying here. Call me if you need anything," answered Ronnie.

When Derek and Stuart got to the hospital, Cameron was in ICU. The family allowed them to go in and pray for him. Stuart's grandmother was there, and he had chicken feet and crucifixes all over his bed and room and was shaking some sort of powder around his bed chanting some mumbo jumbo.

"I'm sorry, but that stuff has no power. Only the blood of Jesus can heal Cameron," Derek told her. Derek removed the chicken feet and crucifixes and swept the powdery substance alongside the wall with his foot. He and Stuart started praying to God for Cameron's soul. Stuart's grandmother rushed out of the room with her hands over her ears when they started mentioning the name of Jesus. They asked God to let him wake up so he can get another chance to give his life to Jesus. They pleaded the blood of Jesus for healing and for God to be glorified through all that he did.

The nurse came in to check Cameron's IV. She told them that the hospital didn't condone the employees sharing their faith with the patients; however, she had been praying for Cameron ever since she heard he was rushed into surgery. "They can tell me not to share my faith in God with the patients, but they cannot stop me from praying. I go in a room by myself and pray. I'll go in the cleaning closet sometimes to pray. I felt a strong urgency to pray for this one. God has a plan for this life. He has the ability to touch many lives," she said.

Derek and Stuart slept in the waiting room waiting for any sign of Cameron to come to. The nurse came over to tell Derek and Stuart that Cameron was asking for them. They could have five minutes with him. Stuart and Derek jumped up and scurried to his room. His stepdad and mom left to give them privacy. Cameron looked up at the two of them standing over his bed and said, "I could hear you guys praying for me last night, but I was so out of it. It felt this peace come all over my body. Mr. Anderson, thanks for coming here in the middle of the night. I have said some pretty nasty things to you and about you. I'm so sorry. Is it too late to give my life to Jesus? He probably doesn't want me now that I refused him earlier. I realized that I really do need him. I thought I was going to die when they bought me in here. I was so afraid, and I couldn't understand anything the doctors were saying. They kept saying, 'We've got to get him to surgery, his blood pressure is dropping.' Me and the guys were just standing on the corner like we usually do, and this dark car came cruising by, and all of a sudden, someone started shooting at us. I know now what Stuart means about going to hell is forever. All I could vision was the devil laughing at me and being tormented forever and ever. Hell seemed so real to me. It was the worst nightmare I've ever had. I've seen scary movies before, but Freddie Kruger, Jason *and* Michael Myers put together in one movie couldn't compare to this. It all seemed so real. I truly thought I had died and gone to hell."

Derek told him, "I never gave what you said about me or to me a second thought. We've been praying for you to give your life to Jesus. I just hate it had to be under these circumstances. You've got to get well so you can tell everyone your testimony of how Jesus saved and healed you."

Derek and Stuart led Cameron through the sinner's prayer. Stuart told Cameron he would come and visit him after school, and since he would be laid up for a few weeks, he would bring him another Bible so he could stay read up.

Cameron had been shot in the upper left shoulder. If the bullet had been slightly lower, he might not have made it. Whoever shot at him meant to kill him dead.

When Derek got home, Ronnie had breakfast ready for him. "I've just got to drop the kids off, and when I get back, we can talk," she told him. Derek called the office and told them to move the staff meeting from 10:00 a.m. to 3:00 p.m. When Ronnie got back from dropping off the kids, she and Derek talked about how happy they were that Cameron had a testimony to share with his friends. "God is so awesome. I was so afraid that Cameron would not make it. His heart was so hard toward the Gospel. I want him to see what God has in store for him. He's so young. I hope he realizes that he almost lost his opportunity to see the Kingdom of Heaven. It's a shame when someone has to give their life on their deathbed and not experience any of the good things that God had for their life while they were alive and well. Just think of all the wonderful years of serving God Cameron has ahead of him," said Ronnie.

Derek and Ronnie took a nap and got up just before it was time to pick up the kids and for Derek to make it to his staff meeting on time. When Derek arrived at the office, he saw Stuart packing up his delivery truck. "I didn't expect to see you today. It could have waited until tomorrow," Derek told him.

"I know. Thanks," said Stuart. "I had to stay busy. I've got so much on my mind today. I'm taking the stuff that's on the way to the hospital. I'll finish the rest tomorrow. I can't wait to see Cameron. I've been thinking about him all day. I am so glad for him. I've been praising God all day."

When Stuart got to the hospital, Cameron looked really depressed. Cameron told him that Trevor was also shot last night, but he didn't make it out of surgery. He was shot in the neck, and the bullet hit that main artery, and they couldn't stop the bleeding. Trevor's mom came to visit him today and gave him the terrible news.

"Why did God save me and not Trevor?" Cameron cried. "I made Trevor the way he was. He was a good kid until he got involved with me. He would do anything I'd tell him. He used to be a good kid and a straight A student, and I got him hooked on drugs. He stopped going to school because he would stay out half the night. I made him steal from his parents. I am the one who deserves hell. I should have listened to you yesterday. Maybe I could have told him about Jesus, and we wouldn't have been on that corner hanging out." Cameron sobbed.

"Listen to me," said Stuart. "Trevor heard the Gospel from Derek at the pizza place and from me. Everyone has their own decisions to make when it comes to salvation. No one can make you give your life to Jesus, and he won't force himself on you either. Just like the decision you made yesterday in front of your house. You told me you weren't ready. It was also up to Trevor both times to give his life when he had the opportunity. Have any of the guys come to visit you? What did you tell them?"

"I told Blaine that I had prayed with you and Derek, and he looked like he wanted to but didn't have the courage. He made a bunch of excuses and left right after I told him he should change his life. I told him he might not have the chance that I had; that he could end up like Trevor next time. I told him I didn't know why God spared me, but I have to find out."

"Well, hopefully, he'll see the light too. I hope he and Jared don't go out and try to play vigilante," answered Stuart. Stuart stayed with Cameron until visiting hours was over. He was being moved to a regular ward because he was recovering so fast. The doctors couldn't believe it. Cameron tried to tell them it was because he was prayed for, and Jesus was healing him, but the doctor told him to get his rest.

CHAPTER 13

IN LOVING MEMORY

It was time for Trevor's memorial service. It was held at the high school. Cameron was not strong enough to go, but Trevor's family allowed him and Stuart to videotape a message to their friends and the family for the services.

Derek allowed Stuart to borrow one of the camcorders, and they made a tape from Cameron's hospital bed. Cameron told the story about how he came to meet Trevor and how Trevor was basically a good kid. He talked about how they all somehow got on the wrong track. He added that if it wasn't for the grace of God, he would be probably lying next to Trevor, and it would've been a double memorial service. He told the crowd that he and Trevor both were told the Gospel at the same time, and they turned their backs on it because they both felt they were too young, and that they would miss out on too much fun. He told them that it was not too late to give their lives to Jesus. He talked about how Derek and Stuart came to the hospital and prayed with him, and he talked about his nightmare of hell while he was out of it. He talked about how he put his pride aside and gave his life to Jesus. He asked all the people that they had vandalized to forgive him and promised to make it up as soon as he got well enough to get a job. He told the girls in the audience that he was sorry for using them and violating them. He added that he was a changed person, and that the next girl he would be with will be his wife. There was hardly a dry eye in the place. He told them that he asked the family to allow his friend Derek Anderson to speak to the crowd, and he wanted everyone to pay attention to the words he was about to say because they may not ever get the chance to hear these important words again.

Derek came up and told his testimony and talked about the day he met these impressionable young men. He talked about how God can change anybody, and it didn't matter what you've done in the past. He offered them the opportunity to come up and have a clean slate. Several people got up and walked out, but the altar was full of teens and adults. At least forty people went up. Derek told them that now they needed to find a church where the truth was being preached. He asked them to choose this day who they would serve. He told them they needed to renounce their involvement with witchcraft because that was of the devil, and God would have no part in it. He told them they couldn't serve two masters. For most of the crowd, it was the first time they had ever been confronted with their unrighteousness.

CHAPTER 14

GUESS WHO'S COMING TO DINNER

The Andersons threw a Thanksgiving feast at the lake house with Millie, members of the church, the office staff and a few of their new friends in Christ. Lake Mystic was beautiful this time of year. The leaves had fallen, and the scenery was like that of a postcard. It was breezy yet unseasonably warm enough for the guys to go outside and play football. Most of them would never admit they were getting too old for this sport (including Derek), but Derek announced he had plenty of ointment and not to forget there was a hot sauna afterwards.

Everyone took time out to give thanks for their blessings around the room and for whatever God had in store for them throughout the coming year. The Andersons stayed the weekend at the lake house along with a few friends who left Friday afternoon. It was peaceful once again after everyone had left. Derek told the kids scary stories by the fireplace while Ronnie made s'mores hot chocolate and baked caramel corn. It was great just having the family together.

It rained all day Saturday, and the Andersons spent the day getting on each other's nerves. Everyone was so edgy from being cooped up. "It must be the weather. We are never like this to one another," Derek said, looking out the window. Just then, he noticed a black Escalade parked down the road under a tree with the flashers and windshield wipers going. "I wonder if they got stranded from the rain. Maybe I'll go over and invite them in for dinner. You don't mind, do you, honey?" Derek asked.

"Of course not, dear. I made enough soup to feed an army. That way there won't be a lot of leftovers." Derek put on his slicker and ran down the road toward the car. He couldn't see inside because the windows had a very dark tint. He knocked on the driver side window, and a strange-looking man all dressed in black lowered the window. "I was…I wonder…me and my family that is…were wondering if you were stranded. We have some nice hot soup on inside if you'd like to come in and warm up a bit. I could call my service too if you're having car troubles," Derek said.

"A nice warm bowl of soup sounds nice," said the stranger. "My wife and daughter went down the road to the general store. They shall be back shortly. Is that your place to the right?" the stranger asked.

"Yes, sir," answered Derek. "When they return, why don't you all come on over to warm up, or I could run and get my SUV, and we could pick them up together."

"That won't be necessary," the stranger replied. "My family loves this kind of weather. Why, it's the most wonderful time of the year. We love the gloom. We came here from Washington State in May. We miss the rain. We're only here temporarily. We came here to check out the business prospects."

"Glad to meet you. I'm Derek Anderson," Derek said, reaching his hand out to shake the gentleman's hand. The stranger had a cold eerie handshake. His hands were thin, pale, and bony. When Derek shook his hand, an icy chill went down his spine.

"My name is Ricluef Krad. My wife is DeMonica and my daughter is Nictasa. Here they come now. I will meet you at your lake house in ten minutes, Mr. Anderson." Derek ran back to the lake house and begged his family not to stare at the Krads. He prewarned them about how strange they were. He never told them how creepy the handshake was though. "Be on your best behavior," Derek warned.

The Krads arrived, and Derek was right. They were very strange. They were *all* dressed in black. DeMonica wore a black hooded cape with a beautiful Victorian-looking black dress that buttoned in the front and ankle-length black granny boots. She had an antique cameo choker around her neck that Ronnie admired and complimented her on. She took it off and handed it to Ronnie to admire. "Go ahead, wear it, keep it for your kindness," she said. "You have beautiful neck for chokers. I have several. They were present from my grandmother. My family was in jewelry business in the old country."

"I couldn't," answered Ronnie. "This is much too precious and expensive to give away. How old is this?"

"That piece…probably one hundred years old," she answered. "If you don't take, I will be offended. Here, let me put it on you." DeMonica put the choker around Ronnie's neck. Her hands were also very cold. "There. Look in the mirror. You are beautiful. Just like cameo." Ronnie looked in the mirror. The cameo was very beautiful on her.

"I will wear it to dinner, and then you must take it back," answered Ronnie. "I don't own any Victorian clothing to compliment such a beautiful piece of jewelry."

"Very well," said DeMonica. "When we open shop in Mystic next week, maybe you find something you like in shop that can go with cameo. Then you keep. I sell vintage clothing. Okay?

"I travel all over the world, collect vintage pieces and sell. Make lots of money. Americans love antiques. We have shop in Maine, Washington, and soon in Mystic."

The Anderson and the Krads sit down to dinner. Ronnie served clam chowder in bread bowls, and for dessert, she had prepared an apple pie. Daphne looked around the table at the Krads. She liked them because they were so unusual. They weren't spooky, just different. Nictasa was sixteen years old, and she wore "funky" vintage Gothic clothing. She had on a black corduroy button-down dress with granny boots that laced up the front and a black shawl to die for. She wore black lace gloves and had on a black hat to match that was adorned with black lace held together with an antique black opal hat pin. Daphne thought she was so cool. Daphne couldn't help but stare. They made eye contact. Nictasa turned to Daphne and said, "I make my own hats and accessories out of scraps my mother gives me of the vintage junk she does not wish to sell. I could make you one if you like. I can make gloves, belts, or almost anything. Just come down to the shop in the Town Square, and I will hook you up."

"Thanks," Daphne replied with a smile. Nictasa did not speak with a heavy accent like her parents. She was more "normal" than they were.

"It is not junk, Nictasa. People pay good money for good stuff," scolded DeMonica.

"Sorry, Mom. You know I didn't mean your stuff was junk," answered Nictasa. She and Daphne smiled at each other.

All the girls went to the kitchen to clean up. "No, you are a guest. You and Nictasa sit at the counter, and we'll talk while the girls and I load the dishwasher."

"What school will you be going to, Nictasa?" Daphne asked.

DeMonica interrupted, "I teach Nictasa at home. I learned to be teacher in old country. People in America make fun of Nictasa. Don't understand our culture."

"Where exactly is old country?" asked Ronnie.

"Romania," DeMonica replied.

Ronnie added, "I am a teacher too. We have something in common. That is so wonderful. I don't work outside of the home anymore, though. I like to sew and cook too. I love taking care of my family. This lake house belongs to Derek's company. We came here for the Thanksgiving weekend to get away from the city life. It feels good to have a place to get away. This is like Camp David for us. The company got us a house in the city, and we have this as a retreat and such. I've gotten so spoiled since I've been here. I worked for the past five years putting Derek through school, and now I can finally relax," Ronnie replied.

When the kitchen was finished, Daphne, Devon, and Nictasa played a game of monopoly with DJ. They had to teach Nictasa. She had never played board games before.

Ronnie and DeMonica prepared coffee for the gentlemen and hot chocolate for the kids. The guys were in the den watching CNN. "It is no coincidence that we meet, Derek," Ricluef said. "I ask around, and they tell me you have best computer company in town. I need computer support to as you say in America 'network' my businesses together. I'm getting too old to travel the way I do. I leave family too much. Time to be family man like you."

"What kind of system do you have now?" Derek asked.

"None," answered Ricluef. "Everything done in ledger book. Have one computer in each store. Records no good. Think manager in Maine stealing from me."

"I can get you a system set up in no time. I will send one of my reps to Maine and one to Washington, and we can have you networked within three weeks. Come into my office on Monday, and we can go over the figures," Derek answered.

Ronnie gave DeMonica a tour of the lake house. They started to bond very quickly. "I marry too young," DeMonica said abruptly, startling Ronnie. "Ricluef come to my father and ask for hand in marriage. Father give me away at thirteen because mother died. I become wife to thirty-eight-year-old man. I know nothing about marriage or anything. He take good care of me like father not like husband. Finally, I go to school to become teacher, but I cannot work as teacher in old country because wife not allowed to work in Romania. I am now thirty-two, and my husband is fifty-seven. I love Ricluef, but I drown self in work in shop because I'm not happy."

Ronnie did not know what to say. "All I can say is pray about it. God will help you find happiness in your marriage," Ronnie replied.

"What do the Gods know? I only believe in self. I be alone since thirteen. I pray to Gods to help me on wedding night. It was night of terror. I know not what to expect when husband come to me. Mother dead, so I have no one to tell me what to do. I feel sick every night when husband come near me. I hate him to touch me. I hate the Gods who don't hear prayer." DeMonica cried. "I have daughter at age sixteen. What do sixteen year old know about being wife and mother?"

Ronnie came over and put her arms around DeMonica. "You need a relationship with Jesus Christ. Has anyone told you that Jesus died on the cross? You need Jesus' love so you can love yourself again," Ronnie told her. She also shared her testimony with DeMonica.

"That all sounds good but too late for me. My life over. Maybe in next life, I find happiness," she said to Ronnie.

"There is no reincarnation, only heaven or hell. You have to prepare for one or the other. When you die, you go to one of the two places. There is no next life as an object or an animal like some people believe. That's all false teaching. We will all stand before God one day and give account of our lives. We will be judged, and then we will spend eternity according to how we lived here on earth."

"I'm very tired, DeMonica," said Ricluef as he stood in the doorway. He startled the women because they didn't know he was standing there listening. "We better start home. We have a nice long drive back to the city."

"You can stay here for the night," said Derek. "We have plenty of room. The girls can bunk together, or we have two spare bedrooms upstairs."

"You are much too kind. We leave first thing in the morning. Thank you very much for your kindness."

Everyone retired to their rooms. Daphne and Nictasa stayed up half the night giggling and talking. Daphne and Nictasa talk about boys and clothes and what it's like going to high school. "I'm so jealous," said Nictasa. "You get to go to school and meet people. My mother keeps me cooped up in the house or the shop all the time. I don't know how to relate to people because my mom won't let me talk to anyone. I sit and stare out the window most of the time. I met a boy once named Trevor. He seemed very nice. When my mom caught him on our porch, I thought she was going to kill him and me. She came after him with her broom. You should've seen him run." She laughed. Daphne told Nictasa the story of Stuart, Cameron, Trevor, and the Mafia Boys. She also gave her testimony to Nictasa.

"That's great you have a God you can talk to. I talk to my dolls all the time. They don't talk back, but I feel better after I talk to them. It's like they understand my pain," Nictasa told Daphne.

Nictasa gave Daphne her gloves, and they decided that when the shop opened, she would visit and make that hat together. The girls finally fell asleep.

That night, Ronnie had terrible nightmares about all the stuff she and DeMonica talked about. She went in the bathroom, got a drink of water and began to pray. She noticed she still had on the cameo. She took it off and put it on the nightstand. She fell restfully asleep. The next morning, the Krads were gone.

"I didn't get a chance to give her back her cameo. It's on my nightstand," said Ronnie.

"Mom, she wanted you to keep it," said Devon. "Why can't you just accept it as a gift?"

"It's just so strange that she would give me such an expensive piece of jewelry having just met me," Ronnie replied.

"They are loaded, Mom," said Devon. "That cameo is probably very expensive, but I bet they probably don't get invited into a stranger's house for dinner very often. I'm sure they were touched that we did that."

The Andersons packed up and headed back to the city. All the way home, Daphne thought about Nictasa and how cool it was to have a new friend. Ronnie kept thinking about how she could reach DeMonica with the Gospel. Derek couldn't stop thinking about the big deal he landed. "This will surely impress the head office in Ohio," he thought. "Networking three businesses together, wow! Let's see, I am going to go shopping for a boat, get Ronnie her *own* cameo, get Daphne a new computer, Devon a new hoop, and DJ, I'll just take him to the toy store at the mall. It's beginning to look a lot like Christmas." (Derek started humming to the tune.)

CHAPTER 15

WHOSE BIRTHDAY IS IT?

It was December 12, and everyone was hyped about Christmas being right around the corner. Ronnie and the kids had decorated the house so beautifully. They found an eight-foot tree that fit perfectly in front of the living room window. They also had a smaller tree in the family room where all the presents were. Normally, Derek would have up his nativity scene with angels singing overhead. Ronnie had asked him several times when was he going to put it all up since it was practically the middle of the month. He would always reply, "I'm too busy. Hire someone to put it all up. You know how it is supposed to look."

Ronnie told him, "It's not the same if someone else puts it up. You used to love decorating for Christmas because you didn't put up Santas and Frosties and junk like that. You've never been 'too busy' for God."

Derek snapped in reply to her, "I obviously can't get any work done here at home in the privacy of my own office with you nagging me." He drove back to work and did not return home until one in the morning. Ronnie and Derek were not speaking to each other. This continued until December 18. Derek would arrive home late every night missing dinner, and when he'd get home, he would go straight into his office and would not come to bed until he thought Ronnie was asleep.

Finally, on the 19th, Ronnie had enough of their family feud. She drove over to Derek's office after dropping the kids off to school.

She stood in the doorway of his office, looked him straight in the eye, closed the door and said, "We have to talk. This is tearing me apart. I can't keep pretending in front of the kids like nothing is wrong. What has happened to us? I told you before I did not move all the way out here to be a single parent. Derek, we are in this together. Whatever I said to make you so mad at me that you can't stand to be around me, I'm sorry. I need a husband around the house. This doesn't work without you. You are my whole life. Let's stop playing these high school games and get to the bottom of our problem."

"I don't know what's wrong with me," Derek answered. "All of a sudden, I have all this rage and anger inside me. It's like I've become a different person. I feel myself not wanting to be around you guys, and when I am, I feel such disgust for the whole world, even all of you," Derek answered. "I think someone has hexed me or something. I don't feel like my old self anymore. I promise, when I get home tonight, we'll talk. Okay? I'm sorry. I never meant to hurt you or the kids. It's this project I'm working on for Mr. Krad. Everything is going wrong. My guy I sent to Washington went over there and had an affair with someone and said he is not coming back to Mystic. When I sent Mike to Maine, he got in a big fight with the guy who was stealing from the company. He thought Mr. Krad sent him to be his replacement. I should have told you what was going on. I've had so much on my shoulders for the past few days. I haven't even thought about Christmas. I've been trying to find a replacement here for the guy who's not coming back because I need to send another guy out there to finish what he screwed up."

"Derek, how could you carry all that and not tell me?" Ronnie asked. "You know I could have come in to the office and given you a hand for a couple of hours."

"I promised you and God that you would never have to work again, and I'm not breaking that promise," Derek answered.

"You must've forgotten we are a team. Baby, you cannot hold things in and expect it not to affect our home life," said Ronnie. "I'm here for you. We are in this together. The kids are going to be spending the weekend with Aunt Millie. Why don't I put in some hours here with you on Saturday, and together, we can try to figure out a solution."

"Okay. I'm coming home soon anyway. I think I can work better in my office at home. Besides, I've got most of my files there," Derek answered.

"I'm going home to start dinner. Remember, it's just you and me. Don't leave me home alone. I'm dropping the kids off at Aunt Millie's right after school. Today's the beginning of their Christmas vacation. She's taking them shopping all day tomorrow. I hope she doesn't wear them out too bad."

Ronnie went shopping for dinner for her and Derek. "I've got to hurry home and make the place all romantic because I've got to take Derek's mind off his troubles. Tonight, he's all mine. Tomorrow, we will tackle this office problem." Ronnie found some stuffed pork chops, one of Derek's many favorites. She ran by the Krad's vintage shop to pick up an outfit for the evening. Ronnie couldn't remember the last time she dressed up for Derek intimately. She couldn't remember the last time they had an intimate evening at home alone. DeMonica helped her select an exquisite black velvet dress that matched the choker perfectly. Ronnie decided to get all the accessories to match. "Derek is going to kill me for spending so much on an outfit, but it's worth saving my marriage," thought Ronnie. The complete ensemble cost $900.

Ronnie dropped off the kids at Aunt Millie's. She hurried home to start dinner. She put the pork chops in the oven and started her bubble bath. She heard Derek came in the door as she was getting out of the tub. Ronnie had set a romantic table for two with fresh-cut flowers and candles. The table was set with her grandmother's fine bone china and crystal like in a magazine. Derek looked around the room, saw no evidence of children and smiled.

"I'll be right out, honey," Ronnie yelled out. "Dinner is almost ready."

Ronnie stepped out of the bedroom with her new outfit on. Derek came out of the kitchen, took one look at her, and his heart started to pound really fast. He ran over to Ronnie and put his arms around her and told her how beautiful she looked. "I must be a maniac to have neglected you," Derek said. "Ronnie, next time I start acting stupid, just hit me in the head with a frying pan or something to bring me back to my senses."

"That cameo looks so good on you, especially since you put your hair up like that," Derek said. "I guess it's because you don't wear jewelry all the time."

"Thanks, honey," Ronnie replied. She was loving all the compliments.

"Is that a new outfit?" Derek asked.

"Yes," answered Ronnie. "I got it at the Krad's vintage shop this afternoon. DeMonica helped me put all this together."

"Remind me to thank her later," Derek said. "You look so beautiful and sexy tonight. Not that you don't look good to me any other time," Derek added hurriedly. "But there's something about tonight; the look in your eyes. You look stunning, honey."

Ronnie and Derek sat down to eat their romantic dinner. It was just like when they were dating. They talked and laughed like old times. It was such a special evening. It was like their honeymoon cruise. Nothing else in the world mattered to them except each other. They did not discuss work or the kids or anything. After dinner, Derek put on some soft music. He reached out his hand for Ronnie. He caressed her ever so gently. They slow danced on the hard wood floors for what seemed like an eternity, gazing into each other's eyes. "I like it when we make up," Derek said while kissing her again softly on the collarbone. The music stopped. Ronnie and Derek just stood there and stared at each other. Derek grabbed Ronnie and hugged her and did not let go for several minutes. "I love you so much," Derek whispered in her ear. "I hope you know that. I know I don't say it enough, but I want you to know that you are my first and only true love." A tear rolled down Ronnie's cheek. She was such a tender heart already, but when Derek whispered such loving words like that to her, it just made her heart melt.

"Do you mind if we skip dessert?" Ronnie asked.

"Not at all," Derek said with a big smile on his face. "We can eat it for breakfast in the morning. You know, it's only 8:00 p.m.? This is the earliest we've gotten to bed in about ten years," he added.

"I'll see you upstairs. I want to slip into something more comfortable," said Ronnie as she approached the bottom stair.

"Don't make me wait too long," Derek said. "I don't want you getting angry because I fall asleep waiting for you to slip into something else."

"Oh, is that what you thought?" Ronnie asked. "You thought we were going upstairs to sleep? I hope you didn't plan on sleeping tonight." Derek ran up the stairs past Ronnie before she could get up them.

Ronnie came out of the bathroom wearing a lingerie ensemble she also got from DeMonica. It was black, silky, and satiny; and she still had the cameo on. Derek and Ronnie started to get intimate, and all of a sudden, Ronnie started growling like a tiger or wild animal or something. She started scratching Derek on his chest like a wild beast. She had a wild look in her eyes. She started tearing away at the sheets and jerking on the bedpost.

"Honey, what's wrong with you!" Derek yelled. "Ronnie!" he yelled, shaking her. Ronnie started growling and howling and laughing in a deep voice. It's a demonic laugh. Derek got chilled up and down his spine like he did when he shook hands with Mr. Krad. Ronnie was sitting on the side of the bed with a wild gaze in her eyes, laughing demonically.

"Do you think I'm beautiful, Derek?" she asked in a deep voice. "Do you want to have some fun tonight while your wife is gone?"

"What do you mean while my wife is gone?" Derek asked. "Who are you? Identify yourself, demon! I command you in the name of Jesus to release her!"

"My name is Cameo, but I am not alone," the demon answered through Ronnie. "There are three of us here, and we are not leaving." Derek laid his hands on Ronnie and commanded the demons to leave her. Ronnie's body jerked, and she screamed in her voice and the voice of the demons. Derek snatched the cameo off her neck and threw it across the room next to the fireplace. Ronnie immediately sat up and asked Derek what just happened. She said she felt light-headed and weak.

"Let's pray right now!" Derek shouted. Derek and Ronnie prayed fervently for a half an hour binding the devil and all evil spirits from their home. They go from room to room binding the devil and commanding all evil spirits to leave.

Just then, the phone rings. It's Pastor Jones. "What's going on out there? Is everything alright, Derek?" he asked. "I started praying, and for the past half hour, I couldn't pray for anything else but for you two. I felt compelled to pray for you two and nothing else."

"It was the Holy Spirit. I'm glad you obeyed it," answered Derek. He explained to his pastor what had just happened to Ronnie and how for the past half an hour they too were praying. Derek spoke with his pastor for another ten minutes getting instructions. After he hung up the phone, he turned to Ronnie and said, "We're going to return these clothes and that cameo tomorrow. I'm also dropping my business deal with them too. I know now that's why my business is going haywire. We'll have to tell Daphne she is not allowed to go over there to make hats either. Last thing we need is for our kids to start tripping. They have enough hell in them."

Derek and Ronnie changed the torn sheets from the bed. Derek got a legal pad off the bureau and started writing the Krad's names. He said, "Ronnie, take a look at this. It's just like Pastor Jones said, "Ricleuf is LUCIFER scrambled. Nictasa is SATANIC scrambled. Krad is DARK scrambled. DeMonica is just plain DEMONIAC," he said. "Why didn't we see it before?"

"We were bewitched, honey," answered Ronnie. "They caught us with our guards down. The devil wants to tear this family apart, Derek. Look at how he had us not speaking to each other for practically a week for no reason at all. I don't know how you feel, but this evening was an evening of lust not love." Derek and Ronnie held each other the rest of the night even in their sleep.

Saturday morning before they went to the office, they drove straight to the vintage shop to return everything to the Krads. They left the clothing and the cameo on their doorstep with a note. "I paid a lot of money for that stuff, Derek," Ronnie confessed.

"That's okay, honey," answered Derek. "I don't want any of their cursed money either. It may cost me a huge bonus, but money isn't everything. We'll survive." When Derek got to the office, he called Mr. Krad to explain to him that he was dropping his networking deal. The Krads were no longer there. The housekeeper answered the phone and said that they packed up and left Mystic around nine last night in a big hurry. She explained to Derek that the Krads were returning to Romania. They had left in a big hurry.

"The devil is no match for the Holy Spirit. He knows better than to mess with God's people. We commanded him to leave, and he did just that!" exclaimed Derek. "He must obey the blood of Jesus."

After leaving the office, Derek and Ronnie put up the rest of the Christmas decorations in the yard. Derek spent the rest of the day putting up the nativity scene with a heavenly host of angels singing over baby Jesus. It lit up the whole block. The media came out to interview the Andersons on their decorations. Derek explained how he was too old to believe in Santa Claus anymore and Frosty the Snowman wasn't real. He told them, "That's for children's fantasies." He also told them about how commercialized Christmas had become. He said, "Whose birthday is it, anyway?"

CHAPTER 16

COMING TO OUR SENSES

Christmas morning came fast. DJ was the first one up. "Wake up, everybody!" Wake up, it's Christmas. Get out the camcorder and watch me open my presents!" he yelled.

Daphne said, "Oh, brother, you would think that after ten years, this boy could sleep at least until eight or nine. He goes to bed at seven o'clock on Christmas Eve and wakes us up at five o'clock!" She went downstairs and started the coffeemaker for her parents. "I hope I have those boots I asked for under that tree," she said yawning.

Derek and Ronnie literally woke up and smelled the coffee. Derek put on his robe, grabbed the camcorder and went straight into the bathroom. "I will get that ugly picture of Ronnie yet to send home. Her friends didn't know how she looked in the morning, but I do," he thought smiling in the mirror. When he came out of the bathroom, Ronnie was already up and sitting at her vanity brushing her hair. "You do it every year!" Derek yelled. Why can't I get that ugly Christmas morning picture of you?"

"You will never be able to pay me back for the picture I took of you three years ago on your fortieth birthday," she answered. "Ever since that day, I put your picture on that T-shirt, you made a vow that you would get me back, so when you get up, I always make sure I get up too."

"Don't worry, I'll catch you, my pretty," Derek replied. "Just remember sick days don't count. I am super ugly when I am sick." Ronnie laughed back at him.

"How can I forget? Hair all over your head, skin all pale and eyes all puffy. You look like the ghost of ugly past!" Derek said, falling back on the bed laughing. "Merry Christmas, sweetheart," Derek said, kissing Ronnie on the cheek.

Derek and Ronnie came downstairs to DJ impatiently sitting on the bottom stair. "Can you two walk any faster?" he asked. "I'm fifteen minutes late opening up my presents. I should be halfway done by now. I know I've got a PlayStation or XBox or something under this tree."

"Okay, son, you can start," Derek answered. "I hope nothing is broke the way you kept shaking your presents for the past three days." DJ opened up the first big box. It has pajamas, a robe, and slippers. The second box has jeans and belts. The third box has three sweaters in it. Derek and Ronnie were laughing so hard because DJ had this half-happy half where-are-my-toys look on his face as he opened his gifts. "Why don't you open this one son?" said Derek. DJ ripped the paper off the fourth box to discover a brand-new catcher's mitt and cleats.

"Wow. Thanks, Mom and Dad!" he yelled and finally found his computer game. Devon was opening her gifts, and she had pajamas, a robe, and slippers also. Her second box has a warm-up suit and K-Swiss sneakers. Her eyes got so big. She ran over and gave her parents a big hug and kiss. The third box she opened has nothing in it but a basketball net. "What am I supposed to do with this?" she asked. "Wear it as a hair net?"

"No, silly," answered Derek. "Look out the window." There is a new fiberglass rim on the garage.

"Oh my gosh! Oh my gosh!" she yelled. "I'm going upstairs right now to take my shower, and I'm going outside to shoot some hoops. Daddy, will you help me shovel the snow and put down some salt?"

"Of course, cupcake," he answered. "As soon as it stops snowing." Devon ran upstairs with her outfit and shoes in her hand.

"She didn't even bother to unwrap the new basketball and tennis racquet," said Derek. Daphne brought a cup of coffee to her parents then started opening her gifts. The first box of course had a robe, pajamas, and slippers. "No boots," she thought to herself. The second box had a black felt hat with lace and an antique hat pin and matching black lace gloves just like the one she was supposed to make with Nictasa. "Just promise me you won't turn Gothic on me," said Ronnie with a smile.

"I promise," answered Daphne. Daphne's third box contained a laptop computer. She always wanted her own computer. No more waiting for the other kids to get off the one downstairs.

With the next box, she hit the jackpot. It was the boots. Black leather calf-high boots. If Daphne didn't open up another present, she was satisfied for the whole year. Those boots cost $300.00. Little did she know her mom got them on sale online for $100 the day after Thanksgiving. They were delivered while she was at school. The kids were all happy and satisfied with their gifts. There were new board games and computer games for the whole family to enjoy. Devon finally found the basketball and tennis racquet.

Daphne had gotten her mom a really cute black sweater and a bath and body gift set. She got her dad a silk tie and tie clip. Devon and DJ bought their parents his and her towels for their bathroom. There was a present under the tree for Millie who would be coming over around three to share Christmas dinner with the family. "I can't wait until she opens it," said Ronnie. "I had a hard time trying to decide what to get her for Christmas, but I think I got just the right thing."

"Mom, Dad, when are you guys going to exchange your gifts?" Daphne asked. "I told your father I didn't want anything but our family to be together and for all of us to come back to our senses for Christmas. I'm content, honestly," she replied with a smile.

Derek came out of the kitchen with a huge box. "Well, Mrs. Content, this is from me," he said. Ronnie opened the big box to reveal a smaller wrapped box, which contained another smaller wrapped box and so on until she had opened six boxes.

"This better be over soon, or else, I won't have Christmas dinner ready," she said. Inside the sixth box was a cameo and a poem. It was just beautiful. Derek had a cameo choker made for Ronnie by a jewelry designer.

"You looked so beautiful in the other one. I wanted you to have one from me this time. Here, let me put it on," Derek said as he put it on her and kissed her neck. "There's one more gift you need to open. Derek handed Ronnie another small box that contained keys to a 2016 Mini Cooper. This is your own private car. No toting the kids around in it. It's for your own personal use. It's in the garage. I had it delivered late last night. "That's what you were up to in the garage? You said you were putting up Devon's rim," said Ronnie. "I heard you pull out the car, but I didn't even pay it any attention."

It was slate blue. It had only two doors. It had a dash cover that said Ronnie's. When they went back into the house, Ronnie handed Derek a gift that contained a captain's hat and nautical jacket. "I know you wanted to buy that boat with your bonus from the Krad's software deal, so I figured this outfit would motivate you to continue on with your dream," Ronnie said.

Derek replied, "Ronnie, I did look at boats, and I saw a couple that I really loved, but I didn't want anything that would take me away from this family again. I figured I'd probably be working on that stupid boat all the time, so instead, I booked the entire family on an Alaskan cruise. If I'm going to be on a boat, I want everybody with me. We will go during spring break. Don't worry about the bonus from the Krad's deal. I got a huge commission because my guys did finish the job, then I let the home office handle everything. I got the money three days ago. I went shopping, and I put a nice allowance in your personal account. I put money in the kid's educational funds also. How do you think I was able to book a cruise for six people and pay cash for a Mini Cooper?"

"You paid cash for my car?" Ronnie asked.

"That's right," Derek answered. "It is paid in full, and because I paid in cash, I got a sweet deal on it with yearend rebates."

"Wait, you said six people. There are only five of us," Ronnie said.

"I know," said Derek.

"You think I'm gonna leave Millie here? She works too hard. She needs a vacation. I already talked to her. She is closing down the B&B and selling it beginning of the year. She was going to announce to the family that she is finally retiring. She says she's got enough money and doesn't see why she can't enjoy life to cruise around Alaska with the family. Besides, she's family, and we are taking a *family* cruise."

"Oh, Derek," said Ronnie. "That is so sweet."

The Andersons ate a light breakfast of muffins and yogurt. It was already eight-thirty, so Ronnie started preparing Christmas dinner. She had to continually kick Derek out of the kitchen because he kept trying to pinch off the ham. "Why don't you go help Devon shovel some snow or something? Make sure there is no ice out there for Aunt Millie!" she yelled, waving her baster at him. Daphne came in the kitchen around one to help her mom by preparing the mashed potatoes and green bean casserole.

"Mom, what are we doing for New Year's Eve?" Daphne asked. "I don't know, but I was hoping to go to the lake house or something," she replied. "Just us this time. Go snowboarding or something. What do you think? Do you want to go to the lake house?"

"I think it would be fun," Daphne answered. "Dad, DJ and Devon could go ice fishing on the lake too," Daphne added. "You and I can stay inside the nice warm house and bake cookies and breads and stuff."

"*You* would like to stay inside and bake with *me*?" Ronnie asked.

"Sure," Daphne said. "Anything but ice fishing. I still remember last year in Ohio. Devon and DJ kept throwing those frozen worms on me. It was disgusting!" They both laughed.

"I've got that on video. I remember it well," Ronnie said. "You were running around screaming because you had a frozen worm stuck in your hair." They both laughed again.

It was two-thirty, and dinner was almost ready. Aunt Millie was ringing the doorbell. She had her arms full of gifts and a cake saver. She'd brought over her delicious homemade red velvet cake, which was a tradition in the Sims family at Christmastime. Ronnie didn't bake it this year. She had no idea that's what Millie was bringing when she said she was making the dessert. It's funny how Millie was keeping the family tradition going on this year. Millie had been baking that cake like Gertie had for years. Ronnie would usually bake it every Christmas too. It was her grandmother's recipe. They had the same family recipe. Ronnie had made it for Derek for the past twen-ty-two years. He was heartbroken when he thought he wasn't having it. Now he was happy again.

Millie had brought the kids some sweaters and socks she had knitted. She gave Derek and Ronnie an old quilt she had handmade and won first place twenty-five years ago at the State Fair. Ronnie handed Aunt Millie her gift. It was a box. Inside were three photo albums of Ronnie, Victoria, and Valerie. It was a scrapbook collec-tion of all their pictures from birth up until last year. Ronnie had copies made of all their childhood photos, high school proms, grad-uations and weddings, so Aunt Millie could see how they had grown up through the years. There were even some photos of Gertie and her mother. Millie was in tears.

"This is probably one of the happiest days of my life. I feel like I did when I first met you and discovered you were my niece." She cried. Ronnie went over and gave her a big hug and kiss.

"I already got a wonderful gift from Derek two days ago," she said. "He called me from the office and asked me about the cruise, and I told him I wanted to go. I haven't been on a boat in years. The last boat I was on I was bidding your Uncle Howard good-bye two weeks after we were married. I never stepped foot on a boat again. I thought I would never see him again."

The Andersons sat down to dinner. "Millie, why don't you stay the night?" said Derek after dessert and games. "It's already after six, and I don't want you driving home. It snowed a little bit more, and I would feel safer because it is so icy out there."

"I guess I should stay," answered Millie. "I've got my new robe, slippers, and pajamas in this box I can wear for the night." They all laughed. Ronnie went overboard with the pajamas this year. Everyone had gotten a robe, slippers, and pajamas. They played more board games and listened to Millie tell fascinating stories about when she was a little girl. Derek made a toasty fire, and they roasted marsh-mallows in the fireplace, and they made s'mores, and Ronnie made her killer hot chocolate to go with it. It was like a Norman Rockwell painting. Everything was picture-perfect.

CHAPTER 17

METAMORPHASIS

"Five, four, three, two, one… Happy New Year!" yelled everyone. It was New Year's Eve, and the Andersons were at the lake house. They even dragged Aunt Millie with them. Derek pulled Ronnie into the kitchen to steal a New Year's kiss in private. "Here's to 2016 and hopefully fifty more," he said. "If Jesus should tarry, that is."

The kids were not looking forward to going back to school on Monday. They were enjoying their Christmas break. It was kind of crazy around the house Sunday night when they got home from church. No one could find any of their things. Finally, backpacks were lined up in the foyer once again. DJ tried to sneak one of his computer games in his, but Ronnie was one step ahead of him. She could read him like a book.

"Awe, Mom," he said. "Everybody is going to bring something to school. How come I can't?"

Ronnie replied, "Why can't I?" correcting him. "Besides, I don't want to have to go down to the school or to someone's house to claim your property. You are too gullible, DJ. We really don't know anything about the kids at your school. It's not like Bradley Elementary. I don't know their parents or anything."

"Alright," answered DJ. "I don't want you mad at me or telling me I told you so either. What does gullible mean?"

"Look it up in the dictionary, and then you tell *me*," Ronnie replied.

"Man, I knew you were going to say that," said DJ.

"You know you can't sneak anything past mom, DJ." Daphne laughed. "One time, I tried to sneak one of my dolls to school, and Mom busted me at the front door. I think she has eyes in the back of her head *and* on the sides!"

Monday morning arrived, and Daphne spotted Cameron and Stuart walking slowly into the school. "That boy is a living testimony," said Ronnie.

"I know," answered Daphne. "They told me last night at church that Cameron is going to ask the school board if he could hold an assembly one morning to give his testimony and show everyone how changed he is."

"Let me put that one on my prayer list," said Ronnie, reaching for her day planner. "If it happens, I want your father in on that miracle. Can you imagine how many kids that would convert with a testimony like Cameron's? Talk about revival in Mystic."

When the girls walked in the door, they saw Cameron with a swarm of girls around him. Daphne was so proud to hear Cameron say, "Look, there is a new kid in school. I left the old Cameron at the hospital. I've been touched, and I don't mean by an angel." He went on to tell them that he was changed by the power of Jesus Christ. He explained that there was no longer a gang called the Mystic Mafia, and the only thing he would be leading was other people to Christ. The girls started walking away disappointed and brokenhearted.

During lunchtime, Daphne, Cameron, and Stuart invited kids to their table to tell them about Jesus and give their testimonies. Cameron and Stuart's testimonies were awesome. They had been living the thug lifestyle for at least seven or eight years. The students still couldn't believe how God forgave all *those two* had done. Most of the school had known them both and was very afraid of them. They had also seen how Stuart would stand up to Cameron and his gang in the hallway since school had started and told him how brave he was just for doing that.

"It wasn't bravery," said Stuart. "I knew that God would protect me, and if something did happen to me, I have the assurance of knowing that heaven is my home. There's this song I just learned at church titled "Blessed Assurance." I know the true meaning of the words. I have a job and a future. I think that I could actually go to college if I really applied myself," he added. Daphne gave her testimony of how she has never drank, partied or slept around, but she would still have gone to hell if she hadn't given her life to Jesus. She explained how the scripture tells that no man can come unto the Father but through his son, Jesus Christ. She talked about sexual immorality and abortion and how the blood of Jesus could cleanse all the pain and hurt and guilt away. She was able to lead three girls to Christ on her lunch hour in one day. The trio decided to go to the office to ask permission to start a Bible club during lunch period since Stuart had after school deliveries. They had asked some students to sign a petition requesting they be allowed to have an area to read their Bible and give their testimonies at lunchtime. It was denied immediately. Principal Green told Cameron he liked him better when he was a hood. He was less of a headache to him because he was hardly at school.

Daphne went home that night and got out her notes she used when she petitioned before the Board of Education in Ohio for a Bible study club during lunch period. In her new petition, she wrote: "We the students of Mystic High School have the right to meet with other students for the purpose of discussing life-changing issues. We also have the right to talk about our beliefs as well as pray at school as long as it does not disrupt school or is not forced upon anyone. It's called Freedom of Speech from our Constitution of the United States. We want to be allowed to be exempt from school activities, movies or book reports that go against our Christian beliefs, and our grades not be affected by our absence as long as we do a *reasonable* assignment in its place."

Daphne presented the signed petition to Principal Green, and it had at least one hundred signatures on it. He looked at her and said, "Every year, I have my problem child. I guess you are going to be it this year."

"I just wanted to show you that we have rights as Christians," Daphne answered. "I'm not trying to be a problem. If you look at my school records from Ohio, you will see that I have been an A/B student for three years, Mr. Green. I'm sorry that I had to present everything this way, but I wanted to show you that I know my rights. All we want is to have a Bible study group during lunch, that's all."

"I'll think about it," said Mr. Green, as he was walking away from her. He would not take the copy of her petition. Daphne took the petition into the office and asked the secretary to send a copy to the Board of Education.

"Gladly," said Mrs. Rupert. "I agree with you 100 percent. As a matter of fact, I want to sign it too. I'll make sure that it reaches their office. I drive by there on my way home. Here, let me get you a hall pass to return to class." Daphne thanked her and went to class.

Stuart's job as courier was getting to be too much to handle, so Derek split the job between him and Cameron. "You would trust me with one of your vans, sir?" Cameron asked.

"Of course," Derek answered. "Jesus gave you a clean slate and so can I. You can start tomorrow. I pay every Friday. It's only $10 an hour for two to three hours a day. Gas the vans up every Friday night and make sure the receipts go to my assistant, Ms. Foster. Stuart will show you the ropes for the first couple of days, and then you should be okay. I get nothing but compliments on Stuart, and I expect the same from you. People who were terrified of Stuart are now inviting him into their homes and not afraid to leave the room or turn their backs on him. I'm proud of him, and I know you will make me proud too. I was thinking after you guys graduate I might be able to get some sales intern jobs for you if you're interested. I know we never discussed if you were going to college or anything, so let me know. I've got a meeting, so I'll talk to you later. Cameron, welcome aboard. Make me proud." Cameron and Stuart just stood there in amazement. Less than six months ago, who would have imagined they would have the responsibility and trust in the community that they have now? Jesus had really done a change in them, and people were starting to notice.

CHAPTER 18

THE ENVELOPE PLEASE

Derek received a letter in the mail on February 1. He was nominated as New Businessman of the Year. The winner of this prestigious award will be featured on the cover of several magazines. There was a grand prize of $100,000 cash, along with a trip to New York City with full accommodations at the Plaza, an awards banquet in the winner's honor in the Rainbow Room, a luncheon at Tavern on the Green, tickets to Broadway shows of the winner's choice, a shopping spree and lots of other amenities.

Derek called Ronnie to tell her all about it. "Honey, you know Millie is going into that assisted living high rise in two weeks," Ronnie warned. "Who will keep the kids?"

"Millie can come and go as she pleases, right?" Derek asked. "Besides, it says that the trip is not until June 10, so the kids will be out of school. Daphne will be eighteen in March and graduated from high school by then. You don't think we can trust her *and* Millie to watch Devon and DJ?"

"I guess you're right," she answered. "You have my blessing. Are you going to reply to your nomination?"

"Now that I have your blessing, I am," answered Derek. "I'm not going to New York without the love of my life, so start getting your wardrobe together."

"I see you have yourself as the winner already." Ronnie laughed. That night, Ronnie made a special dinner for Derek and invited his staff to celebrate his nomination including Stu and Cameron. He announced that night that he was starting a sales trainee program for Stuart and Cameron, and he wanted them to start training in early June. He assigned his two top salesmen to implement a training program for the boys. From that day on, Stuart and Cameron started wearing a suit coat instead of just a dress shirt and tie to work to make their deliveries. They wanted to impress Derek as well as their customers.

Later that month, Stuart announced that he would be allowed to graduate, but Cameron was lacking three credits. English, math, and history credits were not earned from his freshman year. "That's okay," said Derek. "Ronnie is a teacher. Between the two of us, we will have you prepared to take the CLEP exams in April so you can make up those three credits."

Cameron stated, "If they don't pick you for this award, they are crazy, Mr. Anderson."

Derek replied, "By the way, please start calling me Derek at the house. I'm only Mr. Anderson in the office."

Cameron worked hard studying for the next couple of months to earn the extra three credits he needed to graduate. The CLEP exams were scheduled for April 10. Ronnie had assured him that he was ready. She had Cameron over three nights a week and on Saturday afternoons studying and taking practice exams. He had scored 75 percent in math, 82 percent in English and 95 percent in history on the practice exams. The night before the exams, they all prayed for Cameron to pass and to not become confused. Because of Mr. Green's orneriness, he had to take three exams in one day. That was a lot of information to retain. Cameron had faith that God would be with him. He said a silent prayer before he began the math exam. It was tougher than what he had studied, but he passed with 79 percent. Math was Derek's specialty, and he spent most of his time studying with him on that subject. The second exam was English. It was a piece of cake. Cameron aced that one before the time was up and scored 94 percent. English was Ronnie's major, and Cameron learned the most from that through her. History was quite a challenge. Cameron scored only 69 percent. He missed passing by one point, so that meant he was still lacking one credit to graduate. He was so disappointed in himself. He was mad at himself for goofing off and not taking care of business. This would now cost him his diploma.

"Oh well," he said. "I can always go to summer school and make it up. As long as I have a diploma, it doesn't matter to me if I get to graduate."

"Are you crazy?" asked Daphne? "I would just die if I couldn't graduate."

"Of course you would," answered Cameron. "Remember, I was not graduating in the first place. I wouldn't have the credits I have right now if I hadn't given my life to Jesus and start turning my life around. Coming this close makes me want my diploma so much more."

"You're right," said Daphne. "Just lacking one credit is a miracle for you. I forgot all about your past. See how far you have come?"

"Don't worry, Cameron," said Derek. "That trainee job is still yours. Just go to summer school in the evenings and get that credit taken care of. Okay?"

"You still want to give me the job without a diploma?" Cameron asked.

"Of course," said Derek. "I know you can do the job. I have no doubt about that. You have management skills. You were leader of a gang for three years, so I know you can do this. You're a leader. Don't you forget that."

"Thanks once again for having confidence in me, Derek," Cameron replied.

It was Easter Sunday. Time for communion. Stuart and Cameron had never taken communion before. Derek explained to them how it tied in with Jesus' Last Supper in the upper room, and the boys were excited to be a part of it. Easter service was great. Pastor Franks preached on the crucifixion and resurrection and how it was more important than Christmas. He explained that it was the only way to get into heaven, and Jesus' dying on the cross was man's only reconciliation to God. There were visitors who weren't seen since Christmas. Pastor Franks preached about assembling together and hearing the word. He preached on Jesus coming back for his Church and how important it was to live clean and live each day as if Jesus could come back any minute.

After service, the Andersons had Pastor Franks and his family, Millie, Stuart, Cameron, and some staff members to their home for Easter dinner. Ronnie had prepared a feast. Millie prepared the desserts. It was a great day of fellowship.

The kids had a week of spring break, and it was time to take their cruise. Daphne had packed two weeks ago. She had three suitcases. Ronnie made her downsize to one suitcase and a carry-on. "What are you going to do when we go shopping?" she asked. "How do you expect to get all those things home?"

Devon had not begun to pack. Ronnie made her put up her basketball and get packing. Ronnie always packed for DJ because he wouldn't know the first thing to take on a vacation. She made sure he was not trying to sneak any toys in his luggage though. She found a Game Boy and some comic books. She left the comics but removed the Game Boy.

Cameron had a letter from the high school in his pocket for over a week and was afraid to open it. He gave it to Derek and asked him to please read it to him. I just can't take any more bad news. The letter explained that there was an error in the scoring of his history exam by five points. He actually had 74 percent, and he was going to graduate. Cameron was so happy and excited. He said he had to go straight home and tell his mom and stepdad. He was dreading what that letter contained. He had it for a week and had not opened it. All along it was good news.

"That night in evening service during altar call, Cameron's parents went up to the altar for salvation. Cameron had no idea they were even there. They testified that they had seen such a remarkable change in their son in the past six months, and they knew it had to be God's miracle. They told how they were even afraid of their son and would lock their bedroom door at night because Cameron was so violent and full of rage. His stepdad told how Cameron was paying them back the money he had stolen from them and was doing things around the house on his own initiative and how he was working and how respectful he was to them. They knew that the old Cameron would have blown up when he had worked so hard and found out he was not going to graduate, but Cameron came home with such a good attitude and blamed no one but himself. When he came home with the good news today that he was going to graduate next month, they had to come tonight to give God thanks. They admitted that Cameron would invite them to church every time he would go, but they told him they were fine the way they were. The congregation welcomed his parents. Derek and Ronnie invited them over for coffee and dessert after service even though they had to be at the airport at 4:00 a.m. for their cruise. "This is more important," said Derek. Ronnie agreed.

CHAPTER 19

BON VOYAGE

The flight to Seattle was 6:10 a.m. The cruise was scheduled for 2:00 p.m. Millie was not enthused about getting on the cruise ship. She still had qualms about boats. She took her Dramamine, said a prayer and boarded the cruise ship. "I'm not going to spoil this for everyone," she said, although she was dying on the inside to run and not look back.

Daphne was the first one to throw up. She took extra strength Dramamine. She was fine after three hours. The first day was sailing nonstop to Juneau, Alaska. Everyone got a chance to sit at the captain's table during dinner. Derek admired his uniform and said that if he hadn't given his life to ministry, he knew he would've gone into the navy and possibly made a military career or become the captain of a cruise ship. "God had other plans for me though," he said.

"Seems like you made the right decision," answered the captain. "I had a chance to pursue ministry, but I put my career first. It has been one of the biggest regrets of my life. Life on a cruise ship is empty and lonely. Sure you meet people, but you cannot make an impact on their lives like ministry does. Maybe when I retire, I can get back into the ministry. It's too late now."

Derek replied, "That's where you're wrong. It's never too late to give your life to ministry or leading people to Christ."

The captain added, "Do you know what goes on during a cruise? There are lonely, rich women who send me keys to their suites and penthouses every night. There are passengers on board right now who are having affairs. There is drinking and gambling. I cannot be in ministry and be a part of this. I retire the end of this year maybe then I can consider it."

"I think you should pray on it and let God direct you," Derek said. "He will show you where he wants you until you retire. If you like we can go out on the deck and pray together." Derek and the captain pray to God for salvation and direction. The captain thanked him and turned in for the night.

Once the kids and Millie were settled in for the night, Derek and Ronnie took a stroll on deck. It's a cool evening, but Ronnie didn't care. She had Derek's arms around her and enough love in her heart to keep her warm. "Tomorrow, we will take the kids and Millie on a tour and do a little shopping," said Derek. "I signed us up for a tour of an Eskimo village in Ketchikan to see totem poles and a ceremonial dance, and when we get to Juneau, I want to take a catamaran ride to see the whales, sea lions, and porpoises at Auke Bay. If we can fit it in, there is a tour of the Hubbard Glacier, one of Alaska's natural wonders.

"I know Daphne said she wanted some of those furry moccasin boots and a parka."

"I think I'd like a coat too," said Ronnie. "Millie could use a new coat too," she added.

"DJ wants to visit the fishing shops for our ice fishing trip at the lake house next winter," said Derek. I was hoping to do some salmon fishing with him while we are here."

"Great," said Ronnie. "After breakfast, I'll take Millie and the girls and you, and DJ can shop for fishing stuff or rent the fishing boat. We'll meet for lunch and then do some sightseeing until it's time to get back on board." Ronnie and Derek always liked to plan their days ahead of time when they went on vacation.

Derek's cell phone rang. It was Mike, his lead salesman. "Derek, you won the New Businessman of the Year award!" Mike yelled. "You are going to New York in June, boss! Hey, I'm sorry, I hope it's not too late with the time change. I set my alarm so I could give you the news tonight. I didn't want to leave a message on your cell phone. I wanted to give you the good news myself. I knew you would want to know right away. I hope I didn't interrupt a romantic evening or anything."

"Not at all," said Derek. "We were just about to turn in. Thanks for the good news." Derek told Ronnie his good news. They would have to celebrate tomorrow night with the family, then they could ask Millie if she would assist Daphne with Devon and DJ. "We have Daphne's graduation on the 1st then our trip on the 10th. June will be a busy month. By the way, what are we going to get her for graduation since she got the car from Millie?" Derek asked. I thought about sending her home to Ohio for a couple of weeks in July to visit her friends for starters. There are so many people from church that she can stay with. We'll talk about it with her tomorrow."

It was a turbulent rocky night on the cruise ship. Millie did not sleep well. She shared a room with Daphne who dreamed of shopping. DJ and Devon bunked together. They were asleep as soon as they hit the bunks. They fell asleep with the TV and radio on. There were comics all over the floor. Derek and Ronnie came into their room and turned off everything and tucked them in. Derek and Ronnie spent a cozy night on the ship snuggled up, and they spent most of the night talking about how New York would be like a second honeymoon. They wanted to see *Hamilton* or anything by Andrew Lloyd Webber and possibly go to the Harlem Dance Theatre. Ronnie had only dreamed of going to the Rainbow Room someday and dancing with Derek. It was finally coming true.

The tour the next day was great. Alaska was so beautiful. The water was so clean and clear unlike Lake Mystic. They saw moose, elk, and snow dogs and watched the dog races. They got the chance to go inside an igloo. There was a winter clearance sale, and so Daphne got the parka and moccasin boots she wanted. Millie and Ronnie bought almanacs and coats. Devon didn't want a coat, but Ronnie made her pick one out anyway. She also got a pair of snowshoes. They looked like tennis rackets, and that's why she thought they were so cool. She got a hat too. They got free shipping since they bought so much stuff. It would arrive the day after they were home.

Day three was spent touring around Alaska. They went to the wildlife tour and then visited the planetarium to watch the Northern

Lights exhibit. That fascinated DJ. They had the opportunity to watch a ceremonial Indian dance that didn't go over too well with Aunt Millie. She didn't know what they were conjuring up, and she didn't want to stand around to wait for it to jump on her. Millie believed in spirits and saw lots of things during her years in Mystic and never discussed this with the Andersons.

DJ found something on the ground while in the village and put it in his pocket without telling anyone he had it before it was time to get back on the cruise ship.

After dinner, Derek took Millie and Ronnie dancing. They dressed up in evening gowns, and Derek had on his tux. It was ballroom dancing, and the kids were bored. Daphne took Devon and DJ to the game room after their dad gave them plenty of money and told them not to eat too much junk food and to check back in a couple of hours. He warned DJ and Devon to behave for their sister or else.

Thursday would be the last day of the cruise. They would be flying back to Boston from Seattle and taking a charter flight to Mystic. That night, DJ had nightmares and kept Derek and Ronnie up all night crying. He kept dreaming of a witch doctor trying to kill his dad. They were all tied up, and people were going to eat them alive after they killed Derek. Derek asked him what he had been watching on TV, and he said nothing. He then remembered the thing he found at the village and showed it to his dad. It was a rabbit's foot with feathers tied around it, and it had some sort of powdery dust all over it. Derek and DJ went to the deck and threw it overboard. That night, DJ prayed all evil thoughts to leave his mind and repented for taking something that didn't belong to him. Derek explained to him what a talisman was, and he promised he would never touch anything he knew nothing about. The nightmares ended immediately.

It was a long flight from Seattle to Boston. They all dreaded the charter flight after being on the plane for six hours, so Derek suggested they spend the night in Boston and drive to Mystic the next day. Everyone agreed since it was still only Thursday. They had dinner and went sightseeing that evening. They got executive suites at the Four Seasons. It was two adjoining rooms with two bedrooms in each suite, a bar, computer center, and sauna in the room. Derek got a corporate discount, so the rooms were only $400.

DJ and Devon played computer games most of the evening after Derek checked his e-mail. He had several congratulations on being selected for the award. It was really an honor, and Ronnie was especially proud of him. Derek had accomplished everything in less than a year. He was closing huge business deals and had beat Roger's sales record. His corporate office in Bradley sent him news of another bonus he had earned for making their company well-known and recognized. He would be receiving $500,000 from corporate, $250,000 for his own personal use and the rest for innovations awards and to distribute among the staff for their hard work. They were also giving him his choice of a Lexus or Cadillac Escalade for his accomplishments. This was the first time Derek felt he made the right decision of leaving his church and home and moving to Mystic. He always wondered if it was the right thing to do. This award confirmed it for him.

CHAPTER 20

THE GRADUATES

Graduation day had finally come. Daphne was so nervous. "Mom, are you sure there is sim card in the camcorder?"

"Daphne, I'm sure," said Ronnie. "The battery is charged, there's gas in the car, your cap and gown is pressed. What else do you want to worry me about, honey? Calm down. You'll be fine. Your father and I have both graduated twice. It's actually rather boring until you get your diploma. Lots of blah, blah, blah, and then you will all line up to get your diplomas."

Ronnie was absolutely right. The graduation was filled with boring speeches from the principal, superintendent, plus there was the valedictorian speech. Ronnie recorded the entire ceremony but would leave it up to Daphne to edit out the boring speeches. The graduation was dedicated to Trevor Tate. His senior picture was hanging up even though he probably was not going to have enough credits to graduate.

"Honey, get closer so we can get a good picture of all three of them! You are so much better at this than I am," said Ronnie shaking. Now she was the nervous one! As they called Daphne Lynn Anderson, Ronnie grabbed Aunt Millie's frail little hand, and tears rolled down her mother's eyes. She whispered to Aunt Millie, "I wish Mom was here to see this moment."

"She's watching from heaven, dear child," Aunt Millie whispered back at her.

"Cameron Aaron Carter." Cameron got a standing ovation from the crowd. Not only for surviving the gunshot but for graduating. It was unbelievable how he had turned his life around.

"Stuart Daniel Jefferson." Stuart looked so proud accepting his diploma. He caught Derek's eye. Derek being there for him meant the world to him.

They all had lunch at a bistro in the Town Square after the ceremonies were over. The Carters joined them for lunch. Stuart's mom and grandmother declined the invitation.

Derek and Ronnie had a barbecue planned for the graduates in their huge backyard for Saturday evening. Derek had ordered three cakes one for each grad, a ton of different salad plus fruit and cheese trays. He would be doing the barbecuing though. With the help of Cameron's dad and Mike and Steve from the office, Derek had four huge grills going. At least sixty kids from school showed up for the gala. Blaine, who was one of the members of the ex-Mystic Mafia, didn't graduate, but he showed up to wish Stuart and Cameron well. He was ashamed because he did not get the chance to make his parents proud. Blaine stated that his dad was taking back his car and making him go to summer school until he could make up his lost credits. He said he was planning to take the GED test instead during the summer. He would be too embarrassed to go to summer school.

Stuart and Cameron told him about their summer internships as sales trainees at the software company. Blaine was so full of regret. "That could be me too," he thought to himself. "Why did I have to be so stubborn and not go to school? I knew the work. I was just so busy trying to be cool to do it. I didn't want to be a square. Now look at me. I have no diploma; my parents are disgusted with me, and all they talk about is how I should be like Stuart and Cameron."

Cameron replied, "Hey, man, it's not all your fault. I had a part in your demise. I started you cutting class and ditching school. You can blame me if you want to."

Blaine answered, "It's not your fault. I saw the change in you and Stu, and I chose to run with the wild bunch. I can't blame you. You two have done nothing but try to convince me to turn my life over to Jesus Christ. I am the one at fault not you."

He added, "Did you hear about Trevor's mom? She took an overdose of sleeping pills on the last day of school. Trevor's sister came home from school, and found Mrs. Tate passed out on the couch, and the pill bottle was empty and a bottle of scotch was on the table. Mr. Tate's revolver was on the table. I guess she was too scared to shoot herself, so she took the pills instead. She wrote a letter to her family saying good-bye, and she was sorry for not being a good mother because she never tried to straighten Trevor out. She blames herself for his death. She said that if she had been a better mother, he would still be alive. She is on the fifth floor at the county hospital in a straight jacket."

"That's just awful," said Daphne. "I wonder if they will let me visit her?"

"I don't know," said Blaine. "She is out of it, and when she comes too, she talks to herself and screams all day. The reason she's in a straight jacket is because she tried to hang herself the day after she was admitted. My mom checked in on her the other day, and she said she looked wild in the face like an animal. Trevor's dad won't even go visit her. Their Aunt Helena has moved in with them and has taken over as wife *and* mother. The kids all hate her for moving into their parent's room and trying to take her place. She bosses them around all day, and Trevor's younger brother ran away the other day. She slapped him for not calling her mom."

"Is this the aunt that has been married four times?" Stuart asked.

"Yes. Plus she had an affair with Trevor's dad a couple years ago. He took her on a 'business trip,' and Trevor's mom found out about it. Ever since Trevor died, his dad hadn't been coming home like he used to. He has been staying late at the office, and I think the mom caught him with her sister again. She started drinking again, and they would fight every night when Mr. Tate got home."

"What a terrible thing for Trevor's little brother and sisters to go through," said Cameron. "After my dad and my brother died in that car crash and my mom remarried, I would treat my stepdad so bad. I disrespected him, and I would curse at them and threaten to kill them and burn down the house. They were so afraid of me. I used to act like a complete idiot. I would get a kick out of the terror on their faces. I had pulled a knife on my stepdad the very night I was shot. Then I learned that he never left my side at the hospital. When I came to he was holding my hand. He took off from work for almost a month to help my mom care for me after I got home. Sometimes, I am so ashamed to look at him. He gave me nothing but love ever since my mother started dating him. He would take me on fishing trips, and I would ditch him and ruin the whole outing. But he would still plan outings with me. He took me camping once, and I scared him so bad he slept in his truck. But you know what? When I asked him to forgive me after I gave my life to Jesus, he told me that he forgave me every time I would do those horrible things to him. He told me he never wanted to replace my father, he just wanted me to be the son he was never able to have. I didn't know he couldn't have children. When he met my mom, I was one of the reasons he wanted to get married again. He wanted a family. His first wife died giving birth to his only son. His son died three days later. After they were married, they found out he couldn't have children from the chicken pox he got from *me* that left him sterile. He tried to give me all his love for the past twelve years, and I was such a jerk to him. I try every day to make it up to him. We are going fishing at Lake Mystic next weekend, just the two of us. Some nights we sit up and talk about everything. Now that he has given his life to Jesus too, our relationship is so much better. He doesn't drink anymore. My mom is happier too. They wanted me to go to college, but I told them about the sales internship, but I promised them I would take a class or two. I just want them to be proud of me."

"They are, Cameron," said Daphne. "Did you see the look on your dad's face at graduation? He couldn't stop grinning. He's so proud of you. He kept telling everyone how you aced those tests and got your grades up and how you work and go to church. My mom said your mom cried during the whole ceremony, and she said she was so happy her son's life was spared during that shooting. She also said that she knows that God has a purpose for your life."

"It's like a dream," replied Cameron. "I don't know why I was allowed to live. I should've been dead too. That bullet was so close to my heart. I lost so much blood. I deserved death, but he spared me. Why?"

"I think you are like Saul in the Bible, Cameron," Daphne answered. "You persecuted Christians. Now you are a Christian. Have you read the story of Saul of Tarsus? That's definitely you, Cameron. Read it tonight. But to answer your question of why he spared you, that's what you have to find out," answered Daphne. "That is why he created us. It is everyone's purpose in life. First, you give your life to Jesus, then it is up to you to find out why he created you and what his will is for your life. Each and everyone of us was created for a reason, and we have to discover God's plan for our creation. You have to start praying to God to show you his will. Once he starts directing you, then you have to obey his direction. No questions asked." Also what you are experiencing is God's amazing grace."

"What is his will for your life, Daphne?" asked Cameron. "I don't know yet. I have been praying for him to show me and direct me. Maybe it is to be a wife and mother like my mom and follow a godly man. Who knows, maybe I will be a pastor's wife. That would be awesome too. Whatever he has in store for me, I'm ready. I'm out of school, I'm eighteen years old now, and I want to move forward in Christ."

"Do you have plans for college?" asked Stuart.

"Not really," answered Daphne. "I used to, but with all that has happened in the past ten months, I want to just get closer to God and let him direct my path. I know I was put here to serve others, so maybe I could study nursing or something like that. I am supposed to start at City College when I get back from Ohio. I'm going home to my friend's graduation. It's day after tomorrow. I was going to go for a couple of weeks, but with my parents going to New York on the 10th, I'd rather just go to the graduation and come back after a couple of days instead of waiting until July. It's really humid there in July anyway. There should still be kind of springlike weather when I get there. I'll be back on the eighth."

People were starting to leave. All the food was gone, it was starting to get dark, and the mosquitoes were starting to bite. Daphne and Devon started to help clean up the yard. Stuart, Cameron, and Blaine were still sitting in the tree house talking about their futures. Derek came outside with a trash bag, gave it to DJ and joined the guys in the tree house. "There's my boys," he said. "Talking about the future no doubt. I know your heads are full of so many decisions right now. Do I go to college? Do I try to find a wife? Do I try to make a lot of money in a sales career? Am I right?"

"Absolutely, sir," answered Stuart. "I'm just gonna start this training program Monday with a positive attitude and the rest I'll pray about."

"Me too," said Cameron. "I do want to get married someday, but I have to find out what God has in store for me."

Derek replied, "I was just like you guys are now when I was in college. I had so many options. There were several headhunters offering me jobs before I even finished my junior year. I knew I wanted to marry Ronnie, but I also knew she wanted to marry someone who was willing to put God first and then family and then career. That's why our marriage is so strong. She knows God is the head, then the kids, then her, then my career. There's been several times when she has had to remind me that she is not going to be a single parent, and she puts me back on the right track." Derek went to help DJ, and to help the kids clean up. The guys all pitched in too.

Blaine stayed with Cameron for the next two days. He came to church with him on Sunday, but he still wouldn't give his life to Jesus. "I don't know why this is so hard of a decision for me," he explained to Cameron.

"You haven't learned to trust," Cameron answered. "I was just like you. I didn't trust anyone. I had no reason to. But let me tell you lying in that hospital bed I had no one to depend on but Jesus. I was hanging on by a thread. The first two days the doctors told my parents to be prepared to make funeral arrangements just in case. There were no guarantees that I would make it the first forty-eight hours. I remember hearing Derek and Stuart in my room praying for me. There was a nurse who was praying for me too. When she would check my IV, she would touch my wrist and ask God to spare me. When I woke up, the first thing I saw was my stepdad holding my hand; and when I saw the joy in his eyes when I opened my eyes, I knew that something supernatural had taken place in me. I did not feel alone. I felt as though there had been someone watching over me in that room. I could feel the presence of God when Derek and Stuart came back that night, and I gave my life to Jesus. I can't explain it. I know it sounds weird, but I am telling you the truth. Don't be like me and let a tragedy happen before you decide to give your life to him. Stuart had just witnessed to me and Trevor three hours before we were shot. We both told him to get lost. I just pray that Trevor had a chance to get it right with Jesus before he died. Knowing what I know about hell now, it is an awful thought just imagining him being in that place. Total darkness, infinite torture in a lake of fire with the devil laughing at him. We all used to joke about this awesome party in hell. I know now they are not partying in hell. It's the most horrible place to be, and it is forever. Do you understand me, Blaine? Your soul will go there, *forever!* Not just a couple of hours or a week or a year, but forever. Imagine a prison term of life without parole, everlasting and never-ending. You can't hide, you can't run, and the torture never stops. That is a place I never want to go. I just thank God for Jesus. I don't have to go there. He died on the cross for my sins and *yours*. We don't have to go there. There is a way out. Give your life to Jesus, Blaine. Please! Before it is too late. We are not promised tomorrow. We are not even promised the next minute or second. No one knows when death is coming for him. But you can face death with the assurance of knowing that if you died in the next second, you would be in heaven with Jesus. Jesus will only save those who gave their lives to him. There is no other way unto the Father but through Jesus Christ, his son. He is the way, the truth, and the life. We are all stumbling around in darkness until we give our life to him. Let him be the light that guides your path." Blaine still refused to commit to salvation. "Just pray about it," said Cameron. "That's all I can tell you. Ask Jesus to make himself real to you. Start reading that Bible I gave you and wait for Jesus to open the meaning of the scriptures to you. You'll see. He will start revealing himself to you, if you allow him the space in your heart. If you have any questions, you know I'm there for you anytime. If I can't answer them, we'll ask Derek. If he can't answer them, we'll ask Pastor Franks."

Blaine went home that night. He had an uneasy feeling as he started walking home. He ran into one of his old girlfriends, Debbie Mason, at the corner store, and she offered him a ride home. He slipped the Bible in his jacket pocket. Debbie told Blaine that her parents were gone for the evening and invited him over. Blaine went with her to her house. They were sitting on the couch watching television. Debbie got up and offered Blaine something to drink. Blaine asked for juice or soda. Debbie brought Blaine one of her dad's beers. "Since when do you drink juice and soda?" Debbie asked.

"We've got some vodka or rum to go with that 'juice' if you'd like. Relax, I told you that my parents won't be home for hours. It's my dad's poker night, and my mom is at her quilting class until ten o'clock. My little brother and sister are spending the night at my Aunt Judy's. I told my parents I had a major book report to finish, so they let me stay home. They are so square and dumb they haven't even realized that school is out." Blaine popped the can of beer open. He took the can to his mouth for a sip. He couldn't drink it. He kept thinking about what Cameron and Stuart had been telling him about the changes in their lives. He started fidgeting and put his hands in his pocket, but the Bible Cameron gave him touched his hand. Blaine stood up abruptly. Debbie walked toward him and put her arms around his waist and tried to kiss Blaine. Blaine took her arms from around him. He sat back down. Debbie sat next to him and tried to nibble on his ear. Blaine stood up again suddenly.

"What's wrong with you?" Debbie asked. "I've never known you to turn *any* girl away. Why are you acting so nervous? I told you my mom will be home late, not until at least eleven o'clock. Who knows when my dad will show up, and when he does, he'll be so drunk he'll just think you were one of us kids. We have plenty of time to party. It's only nine o'clock.

Blaine remained standing. He did not know what to do; however, he knew he did not want to be in this situation with Debbie. Debbie grabbed Blaine's jacket lapel and pulled him toward her. The Bible fell out of his pocket. "Oh, I see what's wrong with you!"

Debbie yelled at him. "Why are all the gorgeous guys at our school becoming Jesus geeks? Ever since Trevor died, you guys have been scared to live and scared to party. The girls in this town are going to have to date each other if you all keep this up." Blaine stood there still looking at her not knowing what to say.

"If only Cameron were here, he would know exactly what to say to her," he thought to himself. Finally, he said to her, "I've got to go, Debbie. This is not right. I mean, I...I...I can't party with you anymore. I'm sorry for all the times we did in the past. I'm going to start going to church like Stuart and Cameron. I'm giving my life to Jesus before it's too late. I suggest you do the same," he told her walking toward the door.

"Wait!" Debbie yelled. "I can't believe this. You are going to just leave me like this. You're a guy. I know you want it too. You used to always tell me that guys have to have sex regularly, and when they get turned on, there is no turning back."

"That's just it, Debbie," Blaine answered. "I am not turned on. This is not right. I want to start over like Cameron and Stuart. I want Jesus to give me a clean slate like he did for them. I don't want to mess around like this anymore. Do you know how many diseases there are out there? We ought to be thanking God we don't have AIDS or Herpes or something like that. And what if you were to get pregnant? Are you prepared for that? Plus, every person you've slept with I've slept with and vice versa. Besides, Cameron was telling me that sex is for marriage only, it's in the Bible. That's what God created it for."

Debbie turned to Blaine and said, "I don't worry about getting pregnant. My mom does not want to be a grandmother. She's taken me to get an abortion twice. You may have been a daddy already. I just don't know who I was pregnant by. It could've been yours, Cameron's, Jared's, or Trevor's. I got an abortion before Christmas, and I honestly didn't know which one of you were the father."

Blaine did not know what to say to Debbie at this point. He stared at her in amazement. He opened the door and left and walked back to Cameron's house. When Cameron opened the door, Blaine said, "We've got to talk." Blaine explained the whole episode to Cameron.

Cameron said, "We'll never know the truth. Debbie has slept with so many guys at school; I think there were more than the four of us who could have been the father. I'm so proud of you though. You were tempted, but you did not give in to sin. You may as well give your life to Jesus. You are making Christian decisions." Blaine finally allowed Cameron to lead him in a sinner's prayer. They hugged, and this time, Cameron took Blaine home. He explained the importance of prayer to him. He told him about staying in the word. That night, Blaine read his Bible until he fell asleep.

The next day at work, the guys were all hyped up in their first day of sales training. During lunch, Cameron told Stuart all about Blaine and Debbie and the abortions. He asked him why he was not implicated as possibly being one of the fathers, since he had been bragging about being with Debbie too. Stuart told Cameron the truth about never having sex before. He explained to him that he had only gone so far with Debbie and all the other girls but was too ashamed to let any of the guys know that he was still a virgin.

"I'm proud of you, Stuart," said Cameron. "It must feel great to know that you are still a virgin, especially now that you are cleansed by Jesus. You have something that none of us can ever get back. Cherish it and treasure it because it is rare among anyone our age to be out of school and still be a virgin with all the peer pressure and trying to be cool. You and Daphne are probably the only virgins our age left in Mystic."

"I hope not," said Stuart. "Hopefully, there are more. I hate that I had to lie to you and make you think I wasn't a virgin. I always thought you would make me do it as part of an initiation if you found out. I told Derek that you would probably have the guys jump me if you knew the truth. Derek told me that it was nothing to be ashamed of, and I should be proud to be a virgin."

"Derek is terrific, isn't he?" Cameron asked.

"He sure is," answered Stuart. "I'm so glad I followed his girls that night at the pizza place. If he hadn't confronted me, who knows where I would be right now?"

"That's right," replied Cameron. "I know that I wouldn't be gloriously radically changed if it weren't for the two of you praying for me. I just wish I had listened and turned my life around sooner. I regret so many things." Stuart and Cameron loaded up their delivery vans for the afternoon runs. They stopped by Derek's office and talked to him. Cameron told him the story about Debbie and Blaine and how he had a convert now to follow up with. Stuart told him about how Cameron was feeling regret and guilty for his hand in the aborted child. Derek explained to him how the devil used condemnation and guilt to try to spiritually weaken a saint. He prayed with Cameron and had him to ask Jesus to free his mind of guilt and condemnation. Stuart and Cameron left the office to make their deliveries.

Derek's telephone rang. "Hi, Daddy." It's Daphne. She just returned from the graduation with her friend Carla. "Carla wanted to thank you guys for her graduation present. I called Mom, but no one was home. Are they keeping you busy?" Daphne asked.

"Yes, pumpkin. Tell Carla she is more than welcome. Don't stay out too late tonight. I don't want to make Marcus tear Bradley apart looking for the two of you," Derek replied.

"You'll be happy to know that 'Uncle' Marcus is taking us to an elegant dinner tonight. He is not letting us out of his sight. He said that his baby girl is not going out with a bunch of rowdy drunk graduates. Aunt Valerie is taking us shopping tomorrow. Her kids are away at summer camp. She won't see them until Fourth of July. I told her and Uncle Alan all about your trip to New York and your awards. Uncle Alan was so jealous. Aunt Victoria is giving us a tour of her research lab at the university on Wednesday. She is trying to get me to come out here to go to college. She says Carla and I can stay with her if we like. She lives in an empty big five-bedroom house, and she is never at home. She is a workaholic, Daddy. She needs to get married. I told her I was happy in Mystic. Oh, can Carla come back with me and stay for a couple of weeks? Uncle Marcus says that it's okay with him. He's going to call you later on this afternoon."

"He already did, but I was at lunch," Derek replied. "Tell him to call me while you are at dinner, and we'll straighten out the details for Carla. Bye, sweetheart."

"Bye, Daddy!" yelled Daphne.

"Bye, Uncle Derek! Thanks!" yelled Carla.

Derek arrived home and told Ronnie the news that Carla was coming back with Daphne to stay a couple of weeks. The phone rang, and it was Marcus and the girls.

"You taking care of my baby girl?" Derek asked. "Man, I can't believe how much she has grown in ten months," answered Marcus. "Well, I know the girls have already told you about their little scheme to get Carla in Mystic for a couple of weeks; I just had to make sure it was okay with Ronnie. She will be the one putting up with these two. She will fly back with Daphne on Thursday and Regina, and I will come and get her after you guys return from New York."

"We return from New York on June 20, but how about you guys coming for the Fourth of July, and we can take you around and make a long weekend of it, besides I know Carla is not going to want to leave that soon," Derek added.

"Sounds like a plan," answered Marcus. "Take good care of my baby girl until I get there."

"Oh my gosh, can you imagine the two of them together for three weeks? I better load up the fridge *and* the pantry," Ronnie replied. "This should put a smile on Daphne's face for a while to have someone her age to hang around besides Stuart and Cameron. She'll be glad to have another girl around to confide in. She and Carla were so close. I really hated splitting them up, but Daphne understands now how that couldn't be helped."

CHAPTER 21

THE BIG APPLE

Carla and Daphne arrived home on Thursday. They chattered all the way home from the airport as if they had just seen each other for the first time. Derek and Ronnie were so confident that the girls and Aunt Millie could handle things while they were away for ten days in New York. Carla was so impressed with the house. She knew how Ronnie could take any dull room and make it picture-perfect like it came out of a page of *House Beautiful* or *Country Living*.

"Aunt Ronnie, this house is beautiful. I just love Daphne's room. I need you to fly back with me and give my room a makeover. Now that I am out of school, I need a more grown-up look. Daddy says I am not moving out until I get married, so I better make my room look more ladylike than Nickelodean," Carla said.

"Maybe we can all get together for Thanksgiving in Bradley this year," Ronnie replied. "How did your mom like the newsletters I sent her?"

"She loves them. You know Daddy doesn't have time to fix stuff, being so busy at work and the church, so Mom said this was like you being there to help her fix things. She also loved your garden recipes. She made your garden vegetable soup this past winter and brought it to a potluck. Everyone wanted the recipe," Carla answered.

Ronnie and Derek really did miss the Grants. Marcus and Regina (Reggie) were their oldest and dearest friends. They would double date and went out to dinner or get together to play cards or board games. They were very close. Carla was their only child together. Marcus had a son from his previous marriage and so did Reggie. They were both grown, married, and out of the house. Carla was truly their "baby girl." Reggie was told that she couldn't have any more children after her son Royce was born. Royce was a twin. His brother Ryan died at birth. The doctor who performed her Cesarean section almost killed her in the delivery room. He punctured her uterus trying to deliver Ryan, and she was told that she would never be able to hold a baby full term. Her husband divorced her five years later because he wanted more children. Reggie met Marcus at church, and they were married two years later. After several attempts and painful miscarriages, they finally accepted the fact that it was too dangerous for her to try to have another child and gave up. An evangelist came to Bradley for a revival, and Regina went up for prayer for female problems. She was pregnant with Carla within six months. She was sick with what she thought was the flu. The doctor ordered some blood tests and chest X-rays and asked her if she thought there was any possibility that she could be pregnant. She told him about the puncture in her uterus and how she was not able to get pregnant again. The doctor asked her when was her last pelvic exam. She told him a couple of years ago. He then ordered an ultrasound just to be sure before he would do any chest X-rays. The doctor informed her that her uterus was completely healed, and she was three months pregnant. Carla was truly a miracle baby. She was a gift from God.

Ronnie and Derek made sure the family had everything they needed before they boarded their flight to New York. "Make sure you get to church on time. Lock up the house and set the alarm every night," ordered Derek.

"Daddy, I got your list, Mom's list, and Uncle Marcus will be calling every day to check on us. Now go get your award and have fun on your second honeymoon," answered Daphne.

The flight to New York from Boston was not bad at all. Derek and Ronnie had a limo waiting for them at the airport to take them to the Plaza Hotel. Their lavish room was faced overlooking Central Park. Ronnie could see the carriages from her window. "That's what I want," said Ronnie. "A romantic carriage ride through Central Park before we leave New York."

"It's a done deal," answered Derek.

Ronnie and Derek's first day in New York was very busy, and the second day would be busier. They had dinner delivered to their room, and they enjoyed a relaxing evening to wind down from all the excitement. They marked off all the shows they wanted to see. They decided on *Hamilton* and *Phantom of the Opera* for their first and second choices, and they would go to The Dance Theatre of Harlem if time allowed. For attractions, they selected the famous Madame Tussauds Wax Museum, Coney Island, and the Bronx Zoo. There were so many other things to cram in if time allowed. They wanted to see Metropolitan Museum and hear the Brooklyn Philharmonic. Ronnie also insisted they go hear the Brooklyn Tabernacle Choir perform on Sunday. They would not forget the Lord's Day.

The package also included a full day at Elizabeth Arden's for Ronnie while Derek attended seminars and lectures. She was also allowed a shopping spree at Bloomingdale's, Sak's, and Lord & Taylor, while Derek's shopping privileges were Ralph Lauren, Barney's and Kenneth Cole. They had a sitting with Tiffany's to pick out their His and Hers Rolexes, and they were delivered to the hotel safe by security guards. Ronnie had an appointment with Baccarat on Madison Avenue for a crystal and china shopping spree, while Derek was sent to the Manhattan Art and Antiques Center to select pieces for his office renovation. There were so many amenities with this prestigious award of Enterprising New Businessman of the Year. Derek was even being interviewed at NBC Studios for a possible guest spot on the *Today Show*. The awards ceremony was at The Rainbow Room at Rockefeller Center. It was a spectacular evening of dining and dancing. This was the day Ronnie selected to go to Elizabeth Arden's. She had her hair in an updo, and she wore an evening gown and jewels that were "loaned" to her from the Plaza. She selected a champagne-colored satin evening gown from Sak's and borrowed a modest gold necklace with matching earrings. Her matching bag and strappy sandals set the outfit off just right. She looked absolutely stunning. Everyone wanted to meet the woman behind the successful man. When they danced, she could feel all the eyes on her. Derek could feel her hands trembling. He kissed her on the forehead as he always would. "Don't worry, I won't leave your side," he promised her. She smiled at him fearfully never taking her eyes away from his. When the dance was over, Derek escorted her back to their table. So many men wanted to dance with her. Ronnie declined everyone except the CEO of ADT Technologies, Evan Drake.

The evening was luxurious and purely magnificent. Derek eloquently accepted his award thanking Jesus Christ, his wife for putting up with his long hours and missed dinners, his boss, Evan Drake, for believing in him enough to give him the chance to prove himself, and his staff who could not be there but who deserved the award as much if not more than he did. The ceremony was videotaped, so Derek could show his team when they got back to Mystic.

Ronnie wanted Derek to hold her in his arms all night on the dance floor, but the magical evening passed by so fast. It was 2:00 a.m., and Friday was going to be a very busy day; NBC Studios taping, more shopping, lunch with his top execs from ADT at Tavern on the Green, and the carriage ride he promised Ronnie was scheduled for later tonight.

Derek and Ronnie spent their own private day Saturday shopping for Millie, the kids, and their friends and staff. Derek had a plaque made for each of his team members and a huge plaque to display in the conference room with each employee's names engraved on it. He wanted them to know that he truly meant what he said about how much they deserved to be there too because had it not been for their hard work, he would have never won that award. He was going to divide the monies up between his team when he returned also. There was going to be an Innovations Awards ceremony of their own with their families where he would spare no expense for their endeavors. Each team member would get a bonus and a plaque for their innovative accomplishments. They would watch the video of the New York ceremony and then start their own festivities with food, fun, and dancing as well. Derek really knew how to award good, hard work. "Cameron and Stuart will be awarded too. I am so proud of 'my boys,'" he told Ronnie.

Derek had been getting so many good reports on them since they started the internship program. Stuart decided to take a business class during the summer, so he was busy doing that in the evenings. Cameron spent most of his time trying to make up for all the lost time he had wasted not being a part of his family. They took occasional weekend trips together to Boston, Maine, and Rhode Island. It felt good to have his family and the community proud of him.

It was almost time to return to Mystic. Sunday they would attend services at the Brooklyn Tabernacle Church. As much as Ronnie loved being in New York, she was starting to miss the kids and Aunt Millie. She didn't want the romance to end, but she wanted to hug her babies and tuck them in each night. She missed letting DJ read to her at night, putting her to sleep instead of him. She missed her late night talks with the girls. Yes, it was time to return to reality.

CHAPTER 22

THERE'S NO PLACE LIKE HOME

"Mom and Dad are home!" shouted Devon, as she ran out the front door and jumped in Derek's arms like she used to when she was a little girl. Her long legs wrapped around his body.

"Girl, what have you been eating all summer? You are heavy!" yelled Derek.

"All muscle, Daddy. I've been eating my Wheaties, yogurt, fruit, you know, good stuff," she replied jumping down from his arms and kissing him on the cheek. She ran toward Ronnie.

"Oh no, I am not picking you up. You could probably pick me up." Ronnie was very petite. She stood only five feet four inches, and she had a small frame. She wore a size 4 and 5½ shoe. She could pack a punch though. One day, she and Derek were play wrestling, and she elbowed him in the chest knocking the wind out of him. He remembered that day forward to never make her mad enough to really beat him up! Derek was about six foot, and he was medium build but very muscular. He had broad shoulders because he used to play football on the campus lawn and horse around with Marcus trying to play basketball back in Bradley. He had taught Devon to play, and now she was able to beat him with her hands behind her back.

The innovation's awards banquet had finally arrived, and it was held at the prestigious Waterfront Country Club and Garden Terrace in Mystic. They were dying for Derek to become a member since he made Mystic famous. For that reason, they allowed him one of their banquet rooms at the member's price of $50 per person. They would be serving prime rib and lobster, a selection of Italian dishes and salads. Derek demanded that at $50 per person his staff have at least twelve of their own separate banquet servers for a party of fifty. His demands were granted. He special ordered a cake for the occasion from their bakery. It had the ADT logo on it with "East Coast Division: Best Team of the Year" inscribed on it.

Derek had invited Mr. Drake and his family to the banquet also. He had an award of appreciation for him to take back to the corporate office. Plus he wanted to show off his new Lexus to him.

Derek put the Drake's up at the landmark Bismarck Hotel. It was over two hundred years old with deep plush burgundy décor and dark, rich mahogany wood. The lobby was adorned with antiques. The original owner was a German architect who later became a furniture designer by hobby. All the wood was preserved. It also had a "male only" law library/smoking room. It had been that way since the hotel opened in 1873. Feminists in the seventies would protest and hold rallies outside the hotel. It only made the Bismarck more famous.

Mr. Drake was a distinguished gentleman. He had thick silver-gray hair and strong male features with a nicely trimmed beard and mustache. He reminded Derek of Donald Sutherland, the actor. He had studied at Harvard Business School, earning a degree in marketing and finance in 1993, just about the time Derek was dropping out of high school. He had another fatherlike influence on Derek. He took him under his wings and taught him the marketing ropes. He interviewed Derek at Bradley University at a job fair and was so impressed with him that he invited him to interview for one of their sales intern program just like Cameron and Stuart. Derek got very big-headed after he learned he was the only one from the university chosen for the program. Then some of his jealous college buddies told him it was an affirmative action issue. They told him ADT only chose him because they had a quota to fill.

[Derek's mom was half African-American and half white; his dad was Irish and Italian. They met when Derek's mom was a nurse in the military. Derek's dad was a doctor. They were married in Paris. When her tour had ended, Derek's mom decided to leave her military career behind and be a wife and mom for fear they would be sent in opposite directions. Unfortunately, his helicopter was shot down while picking up some wounded soldiers. His mom returned to the States, and she found out she was pregnant with Derek, her only child. She never married again, and she threw herself into her work. She was determined to make something out of Derek's life. She wanted him to be a doctor like his dad, but Derek chose a marketing career instead, then IT and engineering. She was very disappointed because she knew deep down inside that Derek had it in him to be a doctor just like his father. He was very smart, but he ran with the wrong crowd and messed up his grades trying to be cool. When Derek finally came to his senses, he had to get a GED at nineteen.

Because he had dropped out of school, and there were no scholarships for dropouts, Derek's mom worked two jobs doing private home health care on the weekends to put him through his first two years of college. By his junior year, he proved himself and qualified for several academic scholarships, easing the burden off his mother who was in her late fifties and in no condition to be working two jobs.

Evan Drake had been bragging about Derek ever since he got back from New York. It was as if he was the only employee at the company. That made some of his colleagues back in Bradley feel threatened. Whoever followed Derek had some big shoes to fill now. Mr. Drake would expect the same and so much more out of his next appointed executive. There was going to be a new office in San Francisco. No one wanted to try for fear of not meeting Derek's achievements. Mr. Drake wanted Derek to start holding seminars to teach his salesmen how to sell like him. Knowing how much Derek wasn't for being away from his family and traveling all over, Mr. Drake offered to send them to him at Mystic. He even offered to buy him a building to use as a training center, or he could use the lake house and keep it at an informal retreatlike setting. Derek tried to explain to him that it was prayer and putting God first that put him where he was. He explained that he gave his company to God and told him to have his way with it. He also explained that he talked to God about all decisions that were made.

It was a lot to think about. Here was another offer on the table. Starting a training program that meant Derek would have to spend the next few months implementing it, which meant less time with Ronnie and the kids. He knew Ronnie was not going for it. Mr. Drake offered to double his salary. He knew Ronnie was not going for it. There wasn't enough money they could offer to cause him to burn himself out. He knew Ronnie was not going for it.

"Absolutely not, Derek!" Ronnie exclaimed. "Do we need money and toys that bad? When is it going to be enough? We were thinking two years, and we were out of here, right? Isn't that what you promised me a year ago when I said yes to all this?"

"Honey, calm down," answered Derek. "I was just telling you the generous offer Mr. Drake made me. I told him no," he added, kissing her on the forehead. "I reminded him that we signed up for two years, and that's all we want. It's time to start getting ready to head back home. I've recommended Mike to take over for me here. He has a good head for business. He has handled things well in my absence. I hope Drake will give him a chance like he did me. I've put in twenty years with ADT. Only the last five have been full time and look at what I have accomplished. I have the same confidence in Mike."

"Good," she replied. "I didn't move here to *move here*. Understand? Besides, when we go back to Bradley, we are taking Aunt Millie with us. She loves the little senior community she is in, but I am not leaving her here. She goes where we go. We agreed to let her stay there with her friends for another year, and she promised me she would come back with us to meet Vicki and Valerie. I want to take care of her. I can't do it here. Bradley is home to all of us, remember?"

"Ronnie," Derek said. "Look at me. I know you gave up a lot to follow me here. You gave up your Sunday school ministry at the church. You left all your friends and family. Look at what the kids all gave up. But we also must look at what the Lord has done in Mystic while we've been here. Look at all the people's whose lives have changed because we took a chance and came out here. We would have never met Millie if we hadn't come here. I don't regret it. Just seeing what God did in Stuart and Cameron was enough for me. I hate to leave those two. They are like my sons too. I have watched them grow in God. When I go back, I want to have sales positions for them in Bradley. They will have enough training to go back and work on my team. Plus they will make awesome disciples in the Bradley church."

"Do you know how that is going to rip Cameron's mother's heart right out of her chest?" asked Ronnie.

"You be careful, Derek. They are still so young. They can still do a lot for the church here. Don't make them an offer they can't refuse. That would be like stealing converts."

"Yes. Maybe you're right about that. I will offer them to come back with me on a two-year trial basis. That way, if it doesn't work out, there is nothing lost. I will also give them a traveling allowance so they can go back home quarterly."

Derek felt really good about the offer he was going to make to Stuart and Cameron. Did he really believe they would want to leave Bradley once they got there? He was hoping in his heart they would each find a nice girl at the church and settle down in Bradley. He loved these two so much. It was going to be hard leaving them.

CHAPTER 23

GOOD TIMES

The Grants were so excited about coming to Mystic for the Fourth of July weekend. The reunion at the airport was very tearful for Ronnie and Reggie. They've been besties since Daphne was born. When they learned they were finally pregnant, Ronnie would let her and Marcus keep Daphne because Reggie needed practice after seven years of not caring for an infant. As hard as it was for Ronnie, she would sometimes let her baby daughter stay the night with the Grants so they could get a taste of sleepness nights once again. Reggie loved her for trusting her with her one and only child like that. Little did Reggie know, it was a chance for Ronnie and Derek to have some alone time. Having a newborn changed everything in a marriage. As much as a baby is wanted, there is not time for anything anymore. Ronnie was always too tired to go anywhere or do anything. And she certainly wasn't taking her baby in a smoke-filled environment. So they ate take out if she needed a break from cooking. Sometimes, they would plan a weekend "staycation" when Reggie and Marcus had Daphne. It would be a Friday night out of dinner and dancing at the Hilton and Saturday sleeping in for a change. Others would think that was boring, but to Ronnie and Derek, it was sheer heaven.

By the time Daphne was six months old, Carla was born. The honeymoon was over. It was time to return the weekend away favors to the Grants. They even took a vacation together with two toddlers to Six Flags. That was a big mistake. The next year, it was the Grand Canyon without children.

When the Grants arrived at the Anderson home, Reggie stated that it was just as she had imagined. Hearing so much about the place from Ronnie and from Carla's description, it was more beautiful than she had in mind.

"Ronnie, you missed your calling as an interior designer," Reggie said to her. "When you guys move back, you must help me redo the room Marcus had built for me. I'm planning to turn the back of the house into a photography studio. I turned my hobby into a career. I've been doing freelance photography for a couple travel magazines. At first, I was just doing some scenic shots when Marcus and I would go on vacation. Now I'm getting paid vacations to go shoot beautiful parts of the U.S. for travel magazines. Then there was this contest in January, and Marcus submitted three of my prints, and I won second place. First place was a trip to Spain, $10,000 cash and some other stuff. But my prize was a studio makeover with all the latest equipment. Since I didn't really have anything but a darkroom in the back, Marcus expanded the room for me as a Christmas present, and I need you to help me get an office-slash-studio effect going. I have a year to complete the project. They are going to feature my studio makeover in a magazine also. They have already started sending the equipment. I have all the latest lenses. I also got a new digital camcorder she said holding it up, a couple of digital cameras and some up-to-date darkroom supplies. I was thinking hardwood floors and some lighting ideas with some not-too-masculine-looking furniture. I sometimes photograph families, so I need to pretty it up a bit. Would you help me?"

"I would be delighted," answered Ronnie.

"For helping me, I will take you away on one of my photography assignments, if it's alright with Derek," Reggie replied.

"Where have they been sending you?" asked Ronnie. "We've been to Alaska, Hawaii, and Oregon so far. They send me different itineraries, and I discuss them with Marcus, and we decide where we want to spend our vacations. I get three assignments a year. I could have more if I wanted, but I always decline. They want to send me somewhere each month. I have to keep reminding them that I am a wife and mother.

They agreed to our terms, and we get three vacations a year all expenses paid. We do a layout on the hotel and take shots of the surrounding landmarks and restaurants to visit. The hotels always give us the red carpet treatment because they want a four-star rating. We get the best rooms and the best room service ever. We get an expense account to check out the local happenings so we can report it in the magazine article and some of my work goes into a travel brochure. I have a sixty-day deadline when I get back to have my articles ready. The weirdest assignment was to take photos of barns in Oregon. It was for a farming magazine. We had to get up at 4:00 a.m. so we could get the best lighting at sunrise. It was cold, and something in that barn really got Marcus' hay fever going crazy. He was great the whole time. He didn't leave my side. He knows how chicken I am to be alone somewhere I'm not familiar. He is my eyes and ears when I am shooting scenery.

We took Carla with us to Hawaii. That was our second assignment. We only had to pay for her flight. The rest was on the magazine. It's been great. Marcus' staff are so jealous of him. He saves all his down times for my photo assignments. Since he's the boss, he can get the time off in a moment's notice if necessary."

Thursday night was couples only night like the good old days. Derek and Ronnie took the Grants to their favorite restaurant in the Square. Then it was off to the lake house on Friday for the weekend. Millie decided to stay in town where it was safe and quiet. She charmed the Grants. She was just how they described her.

The lake was full of tourists. There was hardly anywhere to lie out on the lake. They mostly stayed at the lake house. By nightfall, there was a spectacular fireworks display by the lake. Reggie had taken three discs worth of photos on the Fourth of July alone. She knew the Andersons would be returning home after Christmas, but she wanted to remember the good time they had in Mystic. Ronnie talked Reggie into making her famous gumbo while they were at the lake house on Saturday. It was a deal as long as Ronnie would make her red-white-and-blue cake for dessert.

"I see how you could get comfortable here, girlfriend," said Reggie. "The lake is a great getaway, and your house is like a picture in a magazine. You guys have really got it good out here. Not that you didn't have it all in Bradley, but you just seem like you belong here. Promise me you will come back home next year."

"I promise," answered Ronnie. "Derek already told his boss that we are not staying. He offered him a great promotion as a training manager here in Mystic, complete with travel and anything else Derek wanted. He turned him down because everything had been moving so fast here. Mystic is a slow town. It is not like living in the city, but everything happened so fast for us since we got here. Derek getting that award has opened up so many doors for him that Mr. Drake is afraid that someone will try to snatch him from under his nose. Derek has had several job offers from Boston, New York, and Philadelphia. He was even offered a job on Wall Street, and he knows nothing about the stock market!

Mr. Drake knows how loyal and trustworthy Derek is. He doesn't want to lose him. Derek has assured him that he plans to retire from ADT in Bradley, Ohio. That made Mr. Drake a happy man. He did give Derek a handsome bonus and a huge raise. He is probably going to accept the full partnership offer when we get back. His income has tripled in the past five years. Derek wants to make sure we have everything we need in case something happens to him. I never imagined he would be such a good provider like he has been for the kids and me. We try not to spoil them too bad, Reggie. I mean that. We want them to grow up to be normal children. Not inconsiderate brats."

The weekend ended too fast. It was time for the Grants to get back to Ohio in two days. Reggie had an assignment coming up in Puerto Rico, and Carla was leaving for University of Ohio in a few weeks. They tried to convince Daphne to come, but she decided to do her first semester at Mystic College to get her feet wet. It was sad having them leave. It was so much like old times doing everything together again. Derek never got the chance to take the Grants to his church in Mystic because they were at the lake.

Ronnie and Reggie took the kids shopping on Monday afternoon at the mall while Derek took Marcus into the office with him. They all had dinner at the pizza place they met Stuart and Cameron.

"I think Carla likes that little Cameron," Reggie whispered to Ronnie. "Look at her giggling and acting all junior high around him."

Ronnie answered, "I think Daphne likes Stuart, but she pretends not to when I'm around. They have been good friends since the day we got into town. The three of them do a lot together. Since Carla came to town, they have been like the four musketeers. You know Derek is trying to bring them back with him to Bradley?"

"Get outta here!" exclaimed Reggie. "That must be why Carla is so giddy. She's only an hour away at the U. I know she will be coming home every weekend now. I won't have to beg her to visit us."

"I don't think that will be a problem at all." Ronnie laughed. The girls looked at their mothers trying to figure out what they were whispering and laughing about. The guys paid none of them any attention. They were discussing upcoming football season while stuffing pizza down their faces. Devon wanted so bad to join in with the guys, but her mom forbid her to be included in male conversation unless asked a question. Occasionally, her dad would ask her NFL questions because he knew she knew all the players and their stats. DJ just sat in awe watching his dad and Uncle Marcus. Derek was truly his hero. He wanted so much to be like him when he grew up.

CHAPTER 24

WRAPPING THINGS UP

September was approaching and it was almost time for back to school. The Anderson's decided not to go to Lake Mystic for Labor Day weekend this year. They went to Salem, Massachusetts, instead for an historical tour. Of course, Millie told them she would not be attending this vacation with them.

When asked by Millie, "Why Salem?"

Derek simply replied, "It will be an educational and spiritual lesson for the kids."

Ronnie added, "Derek's roommate in college did his thesis on the Salem witch trials, and he fascinated Derek with his findings.

They would debate over good and evil. Derek's roommate was intrigued with his findings on satanic cults and their rituals. He felt he could be a leader of a cult. Derek warned him on dabbling in the craft. Derek found out a few years ago that his friend was doing time for murder for practicing the rituals he had become intrigued with. It just so happens that his girlfriend bled to death from something he was trying to do in a spell book he bought at a new age store on fertility. Her family charged him with her death. He is serving twenty years in Ohio."

Driving to Salem wasn't bad, but when they arrived, there was a mass of people. It looked like the remake of Plymouth Rock. Some people were dressed like pilgrims, and some were dressed like satanist all in black hooded cloaks.

Salem was colonial looking just as expected. They attended a mock trial of an innocent family of the 1600s. DJ and Devon stayed very close to their parents this time. DJ promised he would not touch anything nor hide anything in his pockets on this trip. They were waiting to see ugly pictures of witches, but instead only saw people dressed like pilgrims. Derek explained to them that Hollywood portrays witches as ugly and old, but the witches of the sixteenth century were actually everyday people, mostly innocent people, who were suspected of practicing witchcraft.

He chartered a *daytime* tour of their burial places. He and Ronnie did not want to conjure up any nightmares for the kids. As they walked through the cemetery among the graves, Ronnie had a queasy feeling. She kept turning around. She felt a presence as though something sinister or wicked was among them. She felt cold and at the same time warm as though she was about to faint. Derek grabbed her hand and asked her what was wrong. Ronnie could not explain it. "I just feel…weird. Derek, we've got to get out of here. I feel like I am suffocating. All of a sudden, I felt as though I could not breathe," Ronnie says panting heavily. It's like someone is pressing something heavy and hard over my chest constricting my breathing. Aunt Millie was right, we should've never come here. Get my babies and let's go. Now!" she shouted.

As they walked swiftly toward their rental car, Derek and Ronnie both stopped in their tracks. They looked like they had seen a ghost. Located right in the heart of the tourist community, on the other side of the cemetery was another vintage shop of the Krads.

"Hey, look," said Devon. It's the Krad's Vintage Shop. Can we go inside to have a look? We never got a chance to say good-bye, can we stop and say hello?"

"We don't have time," answered Derek. "Your mother doesn't feel well. Let's get to the car immediately."

"What did your father say?" screamed Ronnie. "Get in the car!" The kids looked at each other wondering what's going on with their parents. Ronnie and Derek never told them about the Krads and why they left Mystic so suddenly. After they got into the van, Derek started telling the kids the whole story about that night in December without being too graphic and explicit.

Daphne said, "I thought that hat I got for Christmas came from their shop. I just figured you bought it before they moved away. Where did you find it? It looks so much like Nictasa's."

Derek replied, "I had it made for you by a tailor, honey. I did not want you to have anything that belonged to that family. We didn't want to alarm you kids about that night. It was a nightmare for your mother and me. We wanted to forget it ever existed. Now it's like that demon has come to haunt us all over again. We need to pray." The Andersons began to pray in the van.

They grabbed a quick bite, checked out of their hotel and left Salem. They decided to drive to Martha's Vineyard for the weekend instead. It was packed and overcrowded just like they expected, but it was peaceful and mind cleansing.

The Andersons drove back to Mystic by Monday. Derek set up an important phone conference meeting with Drake for Friday. He was informing him of his decision to leave Mystic in December during the kid's Christmas breaks.

They received a call from the residential home where Millie was staying and discovered she was just rushed to the hospital. Millie did not wish to go back to Bradley now. She learned she had cancer a few months ago, and it had progressed rapidly. She had the same cancer her mother died of, and she refused to be operated on, and she declined chemotherapy. She wanted to be left alone and stayed in Mystic so she can be buried with Howard. Ronnie spent every day with her at the assisted living home where she was now moved to the critical care unit. They read and they took walks when Millie feels up to it.

Ronnie begged her to spend her last days with the family and let her take care of her, but Millie refuses. She didn't want to be a bother or a burden. She told them, "I know what it's like to take care of someone who is dying. I took care of Howard up until the last three days of his life. It was a burden, but he was my husband, and I wanted to spend every moment I could with him. I told him last night I am coming home soon. I will be waiting for him. Pastor Franks has already been by, and we have prayed together, and I have everything in order. I left you and your sisters something in my will. I never got the chance to give you birthday gifts or anything like that, so I split everything I have amongst the three of you. I didn't leave out my grand nieces and nephews though. That scrapbook of pictures you gave me for Christmas helped me get my will in order. I knew then that I had the cancer. I knew when we went on the cruise to Alaska. I wanted to spend as much time with you as I could while I still had strength. Ronnie, I thank God every day for bringing you back into my life. I would have died a lonely old woman had he not given me the chance to know you.

I am so proud of you. You have done a wonderful job as a wife and mother. Gertie would have been proud of you. I'll make sure I tell her how excellent a wife and mother you grew up to be." Millie died quietly and peacefully in her sleep on a Sunday afternoon in September with all her family around her. She had a beautiful smile on her face. She died holding Ronnie's hand. Her last words to her were, "Wrap things up here. Get home and get your sisters converted."

CHAPTER 25

IT'S SO HARD TO SAY GOOD-BYE

Aunt Millie's death was a shock to everyone. She did not tell a soul that she had a terminal illness. She wanted it that way. That's the kind of person she was. So unselfish. She did not want anyone making a fuss over her. She definitely had her affairs in order, though.

She had her funeral arrangements already written up and planned with Pastor Franks. It was hard for him not to tell the Andersons about Millie, but he had to respect her wishes. He had decided that if she got too bad, he would tell them, but she never got to that point. She was a strong woman. By the time Ronnie and Derek found out, it was two months before her death. Millie had no regrets in life. She had done everything she had set her mind to do in her lifetime.

Her memorial services were so crowded that people stood outside. Millie had touched several lives in Mystic. Valerie and Victoria came to the services. It was a great reunion for the three of them. They regretted they had never come to Mystic during the year to meet Aunt Millie when they learned where she was. They were waiting for her return to Bradley. "It's so hard to say good-bye to someone you never got the chance to know." Valerie cried.

"I was so looking forward to meeting her," added Victoria. "I wanted to hear all those stories she told you about her and Uncle Howard. She sounded like she was a fascinating woman."

"Just look around you," said Ronnie, wiping the tears from her eyes. "Aunt Millie was so well-known in this town that some of her regular vacationers at the bed and breakfast even came to say good-bye to her. One couple flew in from Canada. Another couple is here from Chile. They got stuck here on their way to Boston, and Millie put them up for the night. They ended up staying their whole vacation in Mystic thanks to Millie, and they started coming on a regular basis. She had wonderful hospitality. When we first got to town, we stumbled in on the restaurant by accident, and we fell in love with her. Then I found out she was our aunt. *The Gazette* did a spread on us in the family section of their Sunday paper."

Pastor Franks gave Millie a great memorial service. He talked about how much he admired her commitment and dedication to God and to her congregation. He commended her on being there when the young people weren't. He went on to say that his wife and Millie were great friends, and he knew how heartbroken his wife was to lose such a great friend. He also added they started cooking classes for the young women of the church. Millie would demonstrate how to make pie crust, and they started a garden out back of the church and would give gardening tips. [Ronnie looked up at her sisters and smiled.] "That's where I got that from," she said to herself.

Pastor Franks went on to say that amongst all the sadness of Millie passing on, he was most of all rejoicing because Millie had gone home. She would never be in pain again. She would never have to worry about anything because she is with her Heavenly Father. That has got to be the most precious thing in the world. No money, nor fame, nor anything compares to that. Pastor Franks said that he knew that Millie was welcomed with open arms by God because she was such an unselfish person. She would give you her last and not expect anything in return. She would feed the hungry and clothe the needy. There was no charge for Millie's desserts. It was part of the meal. It was her way of saying thank you for stopping by. She would get to know all her customers. She came out to greet everyone. "That's why I have no problem standing here and saying that I know Millie is in heaven, and I know she is wearing a huge crown, and she has heard the words 'well done' from our Lord because she did a great job as a Christian here on earth. She shared her faith with everyone. She was thankful for every day God allowed her to breathe, and she was going to let you know that she was only here by the Grace of God. What a wonderful woman she was and great friend."

Pastor Franks turned the service around and talked about deciding where you wanted to spend eternity. He said, "Millie would have wanted me to tell you this. She does not want you to mourn for her, rather she wants to see you in heaven someday." He talked about how hell is real and how it is full of people who made bad decisions in life. He explained how he had the answer to misery, suicidal tendencies and unhappiness, and that answer was a relationship with Jesus Christ. Pastor Franks did an altar call at the end of the service, and several people raised their hands to accept Jesus as their personal Savior, including Victoria and Valerie. Ronnie was so overjoyed with their decisions.

There was food galore back at the church after the burial. During the repast, everyone had a great story to tell of how they had met Millie and how she had touched their lives.

Valerie and Victoria would be staying in town the rest of the week for the reading of Aunt Millie's will on Friday. The girls all went to the Critical Care Center to gather Aunt Millie's belongings. They discovered she had a storage space she rented not far from the bed and breakfast after she sold it. They found antiques, vintage furniture and old pictures of Millie and Howard when they lived in Ohio. There were pictures of Gertie and Millie too as young women around eighteen or so.

At the reading of the will, Millie left her mink stole to Mrs. Franks. It was given to her by Howard thirty years ago, and she knew how much Mrs. Franks admired it. Aunt Millie also had antiques in storage that she left to Devon and Daphne. She wanted Ronnie to have all her cooking utensils and pots and pans. She also gave Ronnie all her gardening supplies. She gave the church 10 percent of her estate as her tithe to God. Even in death she was still tithing!

Through her sale of the bed and breakfast and stocks she had from some of Howard's investments, Millie's personal estate was valued at over two million dollars. After the tithe was taken out, she willed $50,000 each toward Devon, Daphne and DJ's college education set up in trust funds. She left $10,000 each to Allegiance and Liberty to be set up in a trust fund. Loving Derek as the son she never had, she desired him to start his own company. She wanted $500,000 to be designated to start a software company in Bradley, Ohio. The rest was to be split up between the three girls with Ronnie having one half and the other half split with Victoria and Valerie.

Everyone was overwhelmed with Aunt Millie's wealth and generosity. No one imagined she had so much money. She never flaunted anything, and she lived a modest and content life. She always drove a nice car, but it was never anything fancy or luxurious. She could've been driving a Jaguar but chose to drive a Camry instead. She dressed nice, but she never dressed in fancy high society fashions. Millie was not cheap either. She chose to buy things only if she truly needed them.

Victoria had decided she would devote all her time to her research now that she had acquired her inheritance. It would be great not having to work full time while attending to her medical research.

Valerie decided that she was going to take her family on a long overdue trip, all four of them. Seeing Ronnie and her family she desired that closeness. "I'm going to Toledo, get my babies out of that boarding school, and they are going to a nice private school in Bradley, and I will pick them up and drop them off every day just like Ronnie does. Alan doesn't know it, but he is going to be spending less time at the office too. We are going to be a family again. Ronnie, when you get home, you've got to give me some cooking lessons. If I want Alan to come home at night, I've got to make it worth his while. I don't want him enjoying some other woman's cooking. I stopped cooking ten years ago when we got married. We go out at least four nights a week, and the other nights our maid cooks dinner. When the kids come home, we always get takeout or something. See what you started Ronnie?" Valerie laughed.

"I couldn't imagine not coming home to dinner," said Derek. "Ronnie hooks us up every night. I have to make an appointment with her to take her out on a date. She is very devoted to this household. She has truly spoiled me over the past twenty-two years."

"You deserve it, honey," answered Ronnie. "You work so hard. I never have to worry about bills or anything. Plus, you give me everything I ask for and more. There is no reason in this world why my husband shouldn't come home to a clean house and a hot dinner on time. I don't like my children eating out too much anyway. That way, I can control what they eat and assure myself they are eating healthy nutritious foods. Sure I give them junk food every now and then, but I control how much junk they get."

"Well, since I've been here, I know I have gained at least ten pounds off your good cooking. I've got to get back to the gym (when I get back to Bradley)," Valerie whispered. Everyone laughed.

Early Saturday morning, Derek drove the family to Lake Mystic to show the lake house to his sister-in-laws. "You mean to tell me you have access to this anytime you want?" asked Victoria, looking around in awe.

"Absolutely," answered Derek. "You should have seen the Halloween costume party Daphne and Ronnie arranged for my sales associates and staff this past Halloween. It was a great way for everyone to get to know everyone. It truly broke the ice. We brought Millie to the lake house quite often too. She loved the peacefulness of the lake. I really miss her." Everyone got really quiet.

"Hey, Millie would not want us sitting around moping and mourning. She would want us to be having a good time," said Ronnie. "How about the girls all getting in the pool while DJ and Derek makes us some steaks on the grill?" Just then, the doorbell rang. It was Cameron and Stuart. Derek had invited them to the lake house, so he would have someone to talk to. Ronnie being so preoccupied with her sisters. It was about noon, and the girls were done in the pool.

"I guess we can get in now guys because I know it will be at least five hours before they are done grooming," joked Derek.

"Derek, I don't smell any steaks cooking, honey," said Ronnie. "What y'all been doing all this time? I know you weren't working when you were supposed to be cooking. And you know how hard it is to get you guys out of the pool too."

"Don't worry, honey, dinner will be on time. Guys can swim and cook and hunt and fish and even build a house and still have dinner on the table," Derek replied.

"Oh, I see you are full of jokes today, huh?" Ronnie asked. "Let's see how funny you are when Victoria beats you at Scrabble tonight. You know she is a walking dictionary. I hope she makes you cry with your cheating self!"

Derek turned to Stuart and Cameron and whispered, "She is just jealous because I beat her every time, and she is a school teacher."

Cameron answered, "Derek, dude, you do cheat though. Remember the last time we played at the office? You were cheating big time, man, making up words and calling them countries and stuff."

Derek smiled. "I was just seeing if you guys were paying attention. You know how I hate to lose. I used to play Ronnie all the time when we first got married. Then she stopped playing with me because I would cheat so much. One thing for sure I cannot beat Victoria. I probably won't play tonight because she is tough, and she watches every move I make because she knows how bad I cheat, and she counts the tiles because I sneak and trade them when no one is looking, and I still can't make a decent word!"

Time at the lake house was fun. Dinner was done on time, and Victoria beat the pants off of Derek despite his cheating. They all drove home early Saturday night so Victoria and Valerie could get some rest for church and be all packed before their late Sunday afternoon flight. The airport was tearful, but Ronnie assured them they would all be home by December 15.

CHAPTER 26

MISTY IN MYSTIC

The Andersons spent the next couple of months wrapping things up to leave Mystic. Daphne had begun her first semester at Mystic College and Devon and DJ were back in school until Christmas vacation. The Anderson would be leaving Mystic the 15 of December. They were flying to Ohio to secure a place to live in two weeks. Mr. Drake insisted on setting up living quarters in the executive suite at the Four Seasons for them until they could find a place. What he really wanted was for Derek to remain a partner and become his vice president at the corporate office in Bradley. It all sounded good to Derek, but he also desired his own software company and Millie was making that possible. Drake was afraid Derek would take his clients with him when he left so he wanted to offer Derek anything he wanted to make him stay with ADT. Derek told him he would have to pray about it. If it was going to make him travel more or take him away from his family, he definitely didn't want it.

Mr. Drake assured him that he could work as much or as less as he pleased. He offered Derek a salary of $300,000 with bonuses.

Ronnie spent every day packing a few things they weren't using and storing them in the garage. They couldn't park any of the cars in there for the boxes. They shipped their boxes to a storage facility in Bradley at Mr. Drake's expense. He really wanted to make this transition as painless for the Andersons as possible, but for the meantime the boxes had to stay in the garage.

As she packed the things she got from Millie, she got misty. It was so assuring knowing that Millie was in heaven. She ran across Millie's photo album she had made her and then sat on the cold floor of the garage looking at pictures. She and her sisters had put Millie's old pictures they found in the album. That's where they belonged. Not sitting in a box in storage. It was truly a Sim's Family album now.

Daphne pulled up with her brother and sister and they all went inside for some warm soup. It was already mid-October, and it had started to get cold and rainy.

Derek had started coming home earlier too. He was home at least by 5:00 p.m. nightly. He wasn't fooling Ronnie, Derek liked his dinner hot and fresh. He did not care for food that was kept warm. He knew Ronnie always had dinner ready by six.

Daphne was studying for midterms this week, so she would eat dinner and it was up to her room to study. Occasionally, she would hang out with Stuart and Cameron on the weekend, but since she had started college and they were still training everyone was too busy to hang out that much.

Derek announced at dinner one night that Stuart and Cameron would be coming to Bradley in February. Their training in Mystic would be over late January and they had decided to take a year to work under Derek. Daphne couldn't wait to call Carla and give her the news. "May I be excused?" Daphne asked in excitement.

"Sure," said Derek, "but Carla already knows by now. I told her father this afternoon that they were coming. He's probably giving her the news right now as we speak."

Just then the phone rang. It was Carla. She and Daphne talked and giggled on the phone for at least an hour. Ronnie spoke with Reggie for a little while making plans for their weekend trip to Bradley to shop for a place to live.

The Grants insisted the Andersons stay with them for the weekend and it was a done deal. However, Ronnie informed Reggie that she and Derek would love them to be *their* guest Friday in the Four Seasons suite that Mr. Drake had set up for them. It would be a great getaway for the two couples. The girls could spend a day at the spa and who knows what the guys will do all day. They would treat them to dinner and a night away from it all. They had a double suite for Wednesday through Sunday. The kids wouldn't be flying up until Saturday morning, giving them a chance to look at some houses for a couple of days.

Reggie said she couldn't wait for that. "That must be why Marcus told me to keep all day Friday clear. He and Derek have everything all planned I guess. I will love a full day of pampering and then some romantic time with my husband later," she said. "We don't get out much since Marcus took over at his office."

"Tell me about it," agreed Ronnie. "Derek and I get out maybe once every six weeks, he is so busy. But when we do get out, Derek makes it a memorable evening."

"We will have to agree to get our husbands out more often when you guys move back here. We took that for granted before you left. It seems like Marcus has so many responsibilities and he was always so busy. He came home, ate dinner, then he goes straight to his office and works for another three hours. I always fall asleep waiting on him to come to bed at night. He works too much. With Carla gone I feel all alone in this empty house if I don't have a photo assignment to work on. I was thinking about taking on more assignments."

Ronnie said, "A day at the spa sounds just like what we both need. Don't take more assignments. I will be home soon, and we can do stuff together like we used too, like volunteering at the senior center. Besides I need you there to give me ideas for your studio."

"I guess I can hold out until then. Thanks for cheering me up like you always do," answered Reggie. "I'll see you a week from Friday at the Four Seasons."

CHAPTER 27

YOU CAN GO BACK HOME AGAIN

It felt good being in Bradley again. Everything still looked so familiar, though. Bradley was beautiful in the fall. The leaves had turned
their usual lovely color of bright orange red and yellow. The ground
was almost completely covered with them. There was a crisp, fresh-
ness in the air. It would be hard returning to Mystic after coming
home to Bradley.

Ronnie and Derek looked at several houses. They needed at
least four bedrooms. Daphne would be enrolling at the U for spring
term with Carla and home on the weekends. Devon would be finishing her sophomore year, and little DJ was now going to junior high.
How the kids had grown.

Ronnie and Derek found the perfect house. It looked almost
like Millie's house in Mystic. It was forty years old, rustic and charming. It needed a little work, but that was alright. They would do a
room at a time. Drake had arranged for them to fly back and have all
four cars delivered to them in Mystic. Millie's car was now Devon's,
Daphne and Carla would be using the SUV, Ronnie had her Mini
Cooper and Derek had his Lexus.

The couples enjoyed an elegant dinner, and the guys indeed surprised the ladies with a night out at the ballet. After that it was time
for some dancing of their own. It reminded Ronnie and Derek of
New York, and that wonderful evening at the Rainbow Room. They
all realized they were not spring chickens anymore. It was practically
2:00 a.m. when they got back to the Four Seasons, and they were all

stiff and tired. Reggie and Ronnie spent almost an hour freshening up for their husbands when they returned to their rooms. Derek and Marcus, being the men they were, found basketball highlights on TV to kill the wait time. Both husbands agreed the girls were well worth the wait when their wives came out looking radiantly. Both couples said good night and retired for the night.

Saturday morning the kids arrived by limo at the hotel. Carla also came home for the weekend. They spent the day shopping for the new house, sightseeing and visiting friends. Sunday after church it was time to go back to Mystic. It wasn't good-bye but "see ya real soon." Everyone was so excited that Ronnie and Derek would be returning, especially Pastor Jones.

The next two months went by fast, and soon, it was time to return to Bradley. Reggie, Marcus and Carla had flown over to help the Andersons wrap things up. Cameron and Stuart were getting their good-byes in order too. They would all be flying back to Bradley together; the Andersons and the Grants. Stuart and Cameron came along to help with the move and spend Christmas with the Andersons. You could feel the anxiety in the air. Drake had sent his luxurious private jet to pick them all up. They were traveling in style. The kids pretended they were on Air Force One.

It was a chilly night. DJ never realized how spooky the clouds looked at night. He was the first to fall asleep. Devon fell asleep next watching a basketball game. Daphne was in the bathroom. It was really happening.

The copilot came back to ask everyone to buckle up because they were heading for an unexpected snowstorm over New York. Ronnie became a little nervous. She had never been on a private jet and had never experienced turbulence such as this before. Everyone was very quiet riding through the storm. The captain announces the emergency landing due to ice over the wings.

Daphne thought to herself, "So this is how it ends? I don't get to be a wife and mother?" She took a seat and buckled herself in.

Derek was praying, "Lord, I know you didn't bring us this far to end it like this. I know you are not done with any of us. I'm not accepting this lie from hell."

All Cameron could think about was his parents he just left. He prayed, "Lord let me see my mom and dad again. If it's your will, please allow me to see them one more time. Don't let them go through another tragedy. It would break my mother's heart."

Stuart prayed quietly, "Lord, I wanted to ask Daphne to be my wife for Christmas. If that is your will, please allow us to all live to see that beautiful day. She will make a wonderful wife and mother. I promise I will be the best husband she could ever want. I promise I will treat her like her father would want her treated."

Ronnie prayed, "Jesus, if it is your will, please don't let it end this way. Let us land safely. But if it is your will, I thank you for my salvation. I thank you that my children are Christians. I thank you for all that you blessed us with over the past year."

Reggie, Marcus, and Carla were all huddled facing each other praying and begging God to guide the pilot's hands and guide the plane through the storm. They were thanking him for their family and friends. They were thanking him for their salvation.

There was dead silence. Then a crashing sound as they attempt to land...

One year later...

Marcus was walking down the aisle of the church with Daphne. At the head of the altar was Stuart waiting for him to extend her hand to him. Daphne handed her bouquet to Carla, her maid of honor. Cameron was the best man. Ronnie was standing watching with tear-filled eyes. Marcus kissed Daphne on the cheek and walked over to Reggie and Ronnie and put his arms around them. Everyone sat.

"Dearly Beloved, we are gathered here today..." Pastor Derek Anderson performed the ceremony. He was finally in the complete will of God.

The End.

ABOUT THE AUTHOR

C. L. Holden currently lives in Las Vegas, NV with her family. She has loved writing since a high school creative writing course along with her first job as a page at the library in her hometown in Illinois. She had always been told she had a vivid imagination and decided she should finally write a book with the inspiration from her late mother. She loves to write stories with unpredictable happy endings.

CPSIA information can be obtained
at www.ICGtesting.com
Printed in the USA
LVOW03s2322030118
561718LV00001BA/78/P